THE EARL AND THE COUNTRY GIRL

THE EARL AND THE COUNTRY GIRL

USA TODAY BESTSELLING AUTHOR

EVA DEVON

Entangled Publishing, LLC
644 Shrewsbury Commons Ave
STE 181
Shrewsbury, PA 17361
rights@entangledpublishing.com

Amara is an imprint of Entangled Publishing, LLC.

Edited by Lydia Sharp
Cover design by Bree Archer and LJ Anderson, Mayhem Cover Creations
Cover photography by Period Images, prometeus/DepositPhotos, Mural-Wallpaper/DepositPhotos
Interior design by Britt Marczak

Manufactured in the United States of America

First Edition June 2024

For Mr. Devon and my 3 sons. Whenever there is darkness, you all are my lights. I love you more than words could ever possibly say.

Love is always the way and you all remind me of that every day.

Chapter One

"Promenade!"

Lord Felix Brightman, Earl of Enderley, was not given to following commands. After all, as one of the most powerful men in the land, he was not required to do so.

Yet, when Signore Antonio Morelli said promenade, Felix promenaded.

The Italian fellow was the most sought-after and excellent dance instructor in all of London.

Perhaps all of Europe.

Mamas queued by the hordes to secure Morelli's teachings for their daughters, but it was also important for the gentlemen to learn to dance.

And so he and his good friend, the Duke of Tynemore, promenaded up and down the long hall.

"Turn the leg out, Your Grace," commanded Signore Morelli from his position near the windows, rhythmically pounding his gold-headed cane into the waxed wood floor. The confident and rather intimidating instructor was dressed with aplomb. His clothes were bright and colorful. His hair was arranged in curls that were meant to look effortless but likely had taken hours.

He looked to be an effervescent butterfly ready to take flight. But with the iron determination of an eagle determined that his pupils soar. In time to the music.

In Felix's opinion, dancing was one of the most important skills a gentleman could have. Like so much of the world, he believed in the power of a Renaissance man. Or at the very least, one of the Enlightenment.

Yes, he believed that such a man should be able to skewer a man with a blade and turn a lady gracefully under his arm. *Why choose one thing?* he always reminded himself.

It was no boon to just be able to wield a well-primed pistol. No, one needed a sharp mind and the capability to navigate a room with one's physique.

Tynemore gamboled gracefully beside him.

His Grace was, well, graceful.

Though Tynemore hated every moment at present because His Grace was accustomed to dancing with his wife, the duchess. But said duchess had perished not long ago.

Despite his grief, the powerful duke understood that going to balls and attending affairs was important.

Balls were the sort of events that kept society going.

People thought society was run by the House of Lords and Horse Guards.

It wasn't.

It was run in the beautiful appointed drawing rooms and ballrooms of the *ton* both in town and country. And if one was going to maneuver the outcomes of fate, one needed to have a well-turned-out foot and be able to count to music.

Signore Morelli could assure both things.

"One, two, three, four, turn!" Morelli bellowed and continued pounding his cane upon the floor.

Even with the vigorous instruction and the notes of the

violinist playing the most fashionable tune, Felix could not stop his thoughts from skittering to the letter that he had received this morning from his land agent, Mr. Bilby, in the country.

Bilby was a gentleman, or at least so Felix had been led to believe when he hired the man.

That was how Bilby had presented himself when Felix bought the house in Cornwall, with the fantasy that he would take time away from Horse Guards to go and relax by the sea. He never relaxed, though. He was always at Horse Guards or attending fetes, which would support his needs as an earl and man in government.

The purchase of the estate in Cornwall had been done on a whim, on a particularly taxing day when he had promised himself that a few weeks a year in the sun would be just what he needed.

And yet, he'd never gone. After all, there was always something that needed his attention here in London.

The duke liked to make fun of him for his self-delusions. Felix supposed he couldn't blame him. But the promise, though never kept, that one day he would go to Cornwall, had got him through many a difficult hour.

The duke at present smirked.

"Your face does not match the music," Tynemore drawled under his breath. "This is meant to be a merry dance. And you look as if you were about to start some sort of German march. A dirge does come to mind."

"Well, perhaps it's warranted," he returned, sotto voce, his irritation affecting him deeply. He loathed cheats, even more so if that person was cheating *him*. "I swear to God. I think that Mr. Bilby is filching my purse."

"And what makes you think that?" the duke asked from the corner of his mouth, lest Morelli's fury be ignited.

"The letters, they're so…complimentary." He shuddered.

"Sickening."

Tynemore shook his head, his dark hair dancing playfully over his hard cheekbones. "Ah, a sycophant," the duke observed.

"Exactly, and one must never trust a sycophant." Felix dipped to the music, keeping his shoulders back.

The duke turned out his muscled leg, doing his best to emulate their instructor. "Well, go down to the country and find out what's transpiring, if you're so concerned."

He scowled anew. "I can't just go down there. He'll be a sycophant in person as he is in his letters. But truly, something seems off-foot. I sense that there is trouble there, but I don't know exactly what it is."

The duke shrugged his perfectly tailored shoulders. "Your intuition has saved many a soldier in France. You'd be a fool to ignore it." He paused to turn, then said, "Get away for a bit. The war will not stop just because you go to Cornwall for a few weeks. It would be good for you to get some fresh air, see the country, and sort this business out."

It was true. He couldn't stomach the idea that one of his estates might be in disarray. He liked everything to be in... well, array, so to speak.

He could do it, he supposed. It was an excellent idea, in fact, for his sleep had been disturbed most recently by the unrelenting feeling that all his plans and improvements for his Cornwall estate were being foiled. By a man he was supposed to trust.

At present, he had no solid evidence. But Tynemore was right. The times he had ignored his instincts before had proven disastrous and deadly.

Signore Morelli bellowed once more, "And walk, two, three, four, turn, two, three, four. Clasp the lady's hand—"

Felix and the duke clasped imaginary ladies' hands as they promenaded up and down the long ballroom, their polished dancing shoes easily gliding along the floor, as eyes from the duke's ancestors in paintings along the wall watched silently.

"Go in disguise," the duke said. He pivoted to the tempo of the violin and the beat of Morelli's cane.

"I beg your pardon?"

"Well," the duke began as they turned and promenaded in the opposite direction. "Isn't that what you do in Horse Guards, generally? Tell people what to do, and they do it in disguise in France?"

It was true. He was a man who found members of society who would excel at subterfuge across the Channel to help the English cause in the defeat of France.

He himself, though, was not experienced in the actual doing of such ruses. All of his knowledge was theoretical. Still, the idea of going into the country and putting his knowledge into practical use appealed to him.

A smile tilted his lips as a wave of anticipation rushed through him. Yes, this could be just the thing.

With such a subterfuge, he would also be able to ascertain if Bilby was indeed doing things he should not before the man might hide the evidence.

"It's not a bad idea," he said.

"I don't have bad ideas," Tynemore stated as he bowed left, then bowed right.

"More flourish of the wrist!" called out Morelli.

Felix obliged, giving his wrist a good twirl, before putting his hands behind his back and walking in a circle.

"You should go post-haste," Tynemore whispered as they wove to the right under Morelli's gaze. "You've become sour as of late."

"I have not," he protested, a surprising note of displeasure grabbing his guts at the assessment. He tried to make light of his reaction, weaving left to the sugary notes of the violin.

"You're the one who deserves to have darkness about you."

"Exactly," the duke said, "and yet I find myself swimming along. And you? Well, your face has been growing ever more difficult. I shall have to stop inviting you to my salons and parties," he concluded. "One cannot have such a dour face about."

The truth was Felix was fine. Quite fine. His men were excelling in France, his recruitment of new spies was going well in England. And he was grateful for his purpose.

But he was rather worried about the duke. Tynemore kept acting as if nothing was amiss, as if somehow all would be well, but Felix knew that in private his friend was broken-hearted. The loss of his wife had struck him without warning.

One thing that gave him pause in this adventure into Cornwall? He didn't like the idea of leaving Tynemore, because the man was in complete denial of his grief, which meant it might devour him one day. And Felix should be here for him when that happened.

Still, he could not allow Bilby to go on running his estates if the man was indeed shirking his duties as Felix feared. He couldn't tolerate such a trickster.

Signore Morelli slammed his cane down onto the floor, propped a head on his head, and demanded, "Gentlemen, are we debating in the House of Lords, or are we learning how to dance?"

"Dance, Signore Morelli," he called. "Dance, of course."

"Good," Morelli said, then pursed his lips before continuing. "Because the ladies will be very displeased if you trod upon their feet when you do not know the steps."

He gave Signore Morelli a bow. The man was right, although there likely wouldn't be ladies in Cornwall for Felix to dance with.

But the sooner he sorted out Bilby, the sooner he could return to the ballrooms of London and the ever-pressing needs of Horse Guards and the management of the war in the House of Lords.

If he hated anything, he hated a confident man. It wasn't so much about being cheated himself, but he wouldn't allow the people on his estate to be harmed.

After all, his life mission was protecting the people of England. And that included the people on his estate in Cornwall. If he could prevent pain—for he had seen much pain on the faces of the families of the men he lost fighting Napoleon—he would not cease until it could be done.

Chapter Two

"Might we make perfume today, Mama?" Alice asked, hoping beyond hope that today her mother would say yes.

And yet, as she stared at her mother, whose strained face bore shadows beneath her eyes, eyes made darker by her hair, which was now strewn with shots of silver, hair that was tightly coiled behind her head, without a trace of playfulness, Alice held her breath.

Alice's stomach sank at her mother's exhausted look. Over the years, they had made perfume together. It had been so special and filled her with such joy, those moments when it had felt as if they were transforming simple ingredients into bliss! She'd even learned how to make a scent that suited her and her alone. Her mother had raised her under the careful eye of one who knew the best perfumes in the world.

But over recent years, her mother had retreated further and further from that world.

Alice's spirits dampened, for there was no spark of light in her mother's eyes at the mention of perfume now. In fact, her shoulders sagged as if Alice had asked for the moon.

Once, her mother had trained with her own father, Alice's grandfather, in Paris. He had been a great perfumer there. Lauded, celebrated. Her mother had whispered such things on occasion like temptations to Alice. And Alice longed to know that same sort of greatness. It was almost as if it ran through her veins, that desire to make perfume. She did not seem to be able to eradicate the thought from her head, no matter how often her mother was clear that their work in Cornwall was not in the creation of perfumes, but in the making of tinctures to help the ailments of others, as Alice's father had done.

"No, my dear, no, not today." Her mother sighed. "We must do all of the chamomile."

They had only just finished all of the St. John's Wort. They had corked the last bottle of ointments, and Alice's shoulders were aching. They had spent hours doing it. "But Mama—"

Her mother turned to her and, with kind firmness, asked, "Would you not care for the people of this village? How would we treat so many ailments? Would you tell Mr. Ford that his cuts not be tended to by the St. John's Wort that we have just finished making? Shall we not make the chamomile tea to aid Mrs. Morton in sleeping? Her poor infant keeps her up all hours. She needs to relax. Shall we deny our duty, my dear?"

"Of course not, Mama," she said, her cheeks burning, and immediately set to fussing with the clean linen cloths on the wood table before them, lest her shame at being so artificial cause her hands to shake. Her mother was a good, strong woman who helped so many, and yet she never seemed to look up from the earth to the heavens.

A wave of guilt coursed through her. She could be content. Content to help others. She had to be.

And yet she wished—oh, how she wished—that life could

be a little bit more magical than what it was.

She was grateful that she and her mother had such skills to help the villagers, and as her mother gestured for them to begin the preparation of the chamomile, she swallowed back her silly dreams.

Here in the cozy, clean room of their shop, a room behind the actual shopfront, Alice forced herself to smile. For her mother's sake.

A mother who had given up so much for her children. A mother who never raised her voice and who somehow managed to comfort her youngest children to sleep every night, with a gentle love that seemed impossible given how tired she was. The last two years—since the death of Alice's father—had left her mother haggard. Worn. She'd always been tired, of course, but not like this. Leaving her dreams behind and choosing practicality surely had strained her mother. The loss of her husband, leaving her to do both the child rearing and running of the shop, had nearly broken her.

And yet her mother never failed to make her children feel loved.

She worked so hard, day in and day out, up before dawn and often not going to bed until the stars had been shining for hours in the sky.

"Go and get the chamomile," her mother urged with a smile.

Alice nodded and went to the back of the room, then pulled down several of the dried herbs. She had been doing this since she was small, barely above her mother's own knee. She could do it all herself now.

But they liked to work together, especially when they worked in large volumes.

Some might feel that Alice had become an adult far too soon, but what alternative had there been?

Her mother needed Alice's aid, with so many children

and no husband to help. Her mother needed all the assistance she could get to keep the shop running, a roof over their heads, and food in their bellies.

Life was precarious, and one misstep could see them all on the streets.

Life was terribly uncertain, as Alice's father's death had proved.

Her mother had known that truth even longer. Alice's grandfather had died of a broken heart, himself, and he'd fled France.

He had been a great perfumer, the envy of Paris. But the nobility of France had crushed him. Debt had taken away all his hope, all his joy for the French nobles who were notorious for leaving their bills unpaid.

The great ducs and comtes had bought perfume after perfume, but they had never paid, thinking it a privilege for her grandfather to make perfumes for all of them.

It had broken him, and that was why her mother was so reticent to pass on such a lineage she considered to be only one of heartbreak.

The practicality of making medicines for the villagers was far wiser, despite the fact that sometimes the villagers, after the death of Alice's father, viewed them with suspicion.

Women on their own, without a man to guide them, were often viewed as odd.

Alice took the chamomile flowers to her mother, who smiled and, with bowed shoulders, began working over the petals, picking the leaves, ready to make them into teas and elixirs.

Alice worked side by side with her mother, her emotions a torment of longing building within her, before she paused and dared, "Mama, do you not ever wish…"

Her voice trailed off.

"Wish what, my dear?"

She licked her lips. "That you had opened a perfume shop instead of marrying Papa and becoming an apothecary."

Her mother tensed, then let out a soft, tired sigh. "No, my dear. I would never regret marrying your father and the love that we had or the children that I've born and raised." She lifted her gaze, her eyes shimmering with a grief that had never faded and had yet not consumed her due to the necessity of taking care of so many children. "The only thing I regret is that your father was taken so soon."

Yes, her father being taken two years ago had changed the course of their lives irrevocably. It was a never-ending struggle, making ends meet at home despite the fact that they were needed in the town. Her mother had given up any sort of romanticism, but Alice did not wish for such a colorless life.

From the back of the house, there came squeals and shouts.

Her mother inhaled, resigned. "Your brothers and sisters are at it again."

They always were. Sometimes, Alice wondered if there could ever be a moment's peace in such a house. For her siblings were always playing up. Oh, how she loved them, but they did know how to cause trouble!

Tsking, her mother brushed her hands along her apron, turned, and headed out into the hallway.

Alice gazed at the table covered with all the herbs that would help Mrs. Morton, and so many of the other villagers, relax and know a touch of ease from their overwrought lives.

It was a good thing they were doing. It was noble. Important.

And tomorrow, she would have to go to the lavender fields at Helexton to see if the flowers were ready to be picked.

And then she would go up to the estate to make lavender water, because that was part of her duty, too. It was what allowed them to have land to grow their herbs upon, the deal her mother had made with Helexton's estate agent, Mr. Bilby.

And yet, oh, how she longed for more, just a bit more. A grander life than this one that did not bear the same repetition day in and day out.

The shouting in the other room stopped, and her mama reentered the kitchen with a bemused expression. "We should send them to France. They'd never stand a chance against your brother's determined spirit. But perhaps they shall one day learn peace over bickering. Just like our countries, eh? Long live peace?"

"I don't know, Mama," Alice groaned, giving her mother a smile. "I'm not entirely sure that Samuel and Paul know how to do anything but bicker."

Her mother laughed fully. "You are right, of course. Now, my dear, go and get the oil. We shall make a cordial first."

Alice nodded, glad to see her mother laugh and smile.

She supposed this was a good life.

And yet her heart, her infuriating heart, whispered for something exciting to happen. Anything. Anything at all.

Something that would make her dreams a reality and not just a longing in her heart.

Chapter Three

"Get your hands off my lavender, good sir," a woman called from behind him.

Felix straightened, stunned by the tone. He was not accustomed to being spoken to thus. The voice was quite startling, and the demand was absurd for an earl.

He whirled around to locate the owner of said voice and was shocked to find that the young woman was standing right near him.

Or she had been. But now she staggered back from his quick movement, her eyes flared, and she lost her footing.

He caught her instinctively, but the two of them went down into the field in an eruption of lavender blossoms. The scent of earth and vibrant flowers enveloped them.

"Devil take it!" she exclaimed. "Now your hands are on *me*." She paused as if waiting for him to do something. "You should get them off."

She was absolutely right.

He should get his hands off this young woman. But here, in the lavender field with purple petals floating about them and landing on them, he felt in complete disarray.

It was not his usual state of affairs. In fact, he was the one who usually put others in disarray.

He was a man of remarkable composure. Or so he prided himself.

"Forgive me," he said, trying to remember to keep his voice not as aristocratic as it usually was. After all, he was here in disguise. Not the hat and false mustache kind, of course. This was different but still essential.

He was not supposed to be the Earl of Enderley here. This was not his lavender field.

He owned it. Of course he did. All of the land as far as the eye could see was his. All part of the estate he'd bought on that promise to himself of a bit of warmth and rest.

But he was a man of determined action, and Napoleon was raging on the continent. No, he spent all of his time recruiting young men to be spies in France and to make certain the war was going as it should.

Still, needs must, and the exposure of his land agent had to be done.

Yes, Felix was here to make certain that he was correct in his assumptions. He'd come disguised as a stable master who specialized in thoroughbreds to ascertain what was truly happening on his lands. It was made possible by the fact that he had never visited the property. Not once. He'd bought it purely based on a description.

He could not let the young woman in his arms know who he truly was, hence his need to keep his voice rough. And as he gazed down at her, he realized she was positively surprised but not horrified. She was staring up at him, her eyes violet, which seemed to match her lavender field, gazing upon him with wonder.

"Excuse me," she clarified archly, "but what the blazes are you doing here? And your hands are still upon me."

He frowned. So they were.

He pulled back, stood, and helped her up as well, though he realized how very much he'd liked the feel of her beneath him. The soft curve of her body when it had been pressed into his and the intoxicating scent of the lavender around them was quite overwhelming.

He studied her carefully, from the top of her blond, curly head to those wide, shocking eyes. Her nose was pert. Her mouth looked ready to set him down, which he absolutely adored. Her chin was elfin, pointed. One might have thought she was actually rather austere-looking, like she would be best suited in a crowded hall, demanding rights for women, refusing to be shouted down by red-faced parliamentarians.

He rather liked the idea of that, too.

He leaned back further, and she drew in a long breath. Her chest rose, and he noted the curve of her breasts pressed against the cut of her simple cotton gown.

It was quite the sight, but he was a gentleman, even if she was not to know that, and he would not be playing the rogue.

"Do forgive me, miss," he said. "I was simply caught off guard. You have quite a striking voice."

She laughed. "Yes, well, one needs a striking voice when one works in the fields."

"You work in the fields?" he asked, hardly believing such a claim, stunned by the effect her laugh had on his person. That lush, rolling bell of sound had cause his skin to awaken and his body to tighten in the most delicious of ways.

He eyed her. She did not look like the sort of person who cut wheat or collected vegetables. "Do you take in the cabbage or something?"

She laughed again, a refreshing sound that was not manufactured for the delectation of lords. No, it was a full, throaty laugh that carried. Much like her voice.

She scooted away, then eyed him as if he was a fox that

had got in her hen house and planned to make short work of him. "No, the lavender fields. They are my mother's. And of course the apples, the pears, the freesia, a remarkable variety of flowers and herbs." She brushed her hands together, removing the soil from them, and scanned the horizon. "Not all of them are in bloom at present."

"I see," he said. "Your family owns them."

"Well," she rolled her eyes, "of course we don't actually *own* the fields. The only person who owns anything around here is the Earl of Enderley. He owns the estate Helexton."

"Oh, does he, then?" he asked, trying to keep his face calm. "Well, then I must be in the right place."

Her eyebrows darted up. "What do you mean?"

"I am his latest man of stables."

"Oh," she said, her brow furrowing as she took him in again. "That might explain why you're so entirely lost. Did no one give you direction in the town?"

He grinned. "I must admit I was rather arrogant and assumed I would be able to find it. And as I was going down this road, I spotted your beautiful field and felt the need to, well, examine it."

"Very ill done of you, sir," she tsked. "You have squashed all of these flowers."

"I correct you," he said, his lips curving. He couldn't stop himself. "*We* have squashed the flowers."

She groaned. "Oh dear," she said. "Are you one of those?"

"One of what?" he asked, wondering if he should be offended.

She snorted. "A literalist."

"Ah," he began, relieved. "Words matter."

She scowled at him. "Words do matter," she agreed impatiently, "but they can't replace my flowers."

He winced inwardly. "I'm very sorry. It was badly done of me. I didn't know I was causing harm. I merely wished to admire them. They're very beautiful."

"They are," she said, her voice softening as she gazed around at the petals and the acres of lavender plants.

"Whatever do you do with them?" he asked, scanning the flowers dancing under the sun. "It's a vast amount of flowers. Do you make up ladies' bouquets for the ton or weddings?"

She rolled her eyes. "Absolutely not. I've never even been to London. I cannot imagine my flowers going there, donning ballrooms."

"You can't?" he asked, skeptical, for the flowers were of quality. "I'm sure ladies would want them. They would be in high demand."

They stared at each other for several long moments, each moment ensuring him she might never forgive him for the squashing of her plants.

At long last, he ventured, "Can you direct me to the house of the estate?"

"Of course I can," she said, pivoting on her boot. "Come along then, I'll take you where you are supposed to go. I suppose I can take a little bit of time out of my day to be of assistance."

He hid a smile. There was something about her manner that he found quite endearing. "Very good of you, Miss…"

She turned back and propped a hand upon her hip, "Miss Alice Wright."

"Your name is Miss *Wright*?"

"Indeed."

He wanted to laugh but did not. Surely, fate would not play with him thus. He did not have a Miss *Right* in his plan. There was no Lady *Right*, either.

One day he would marry, of course. He was required to do so. He had to produce an heir. But he would never, ever choose a woman like Miss Wright.

No one so effervescent, no one so clever, no one so beautiful, no one so interesting, and no one who looked like she could glare at him and have her way with him verbally, mentally, and physically in a trice. And the main reason was he wanted to make absolutely certain that he had no emotional attachment to the woman he married.

He had learned a very long time ago, after sending countless letters to widows, that love was the cruelest thing in the world. Love destroyed people. It burned them down. It broke them apart, and so he had no wish to fall in love. He'd seen too many broken-hearted people left behind.

But Miss Wright was quite something, and there was no denying that.

He spotted something amiss, and before he could stop himself, he slowly reached out to her. The air seemed to still and the world to stop as his breath hitched in his throat at his daring.

"What are you doing?" she said, eyeing him carefully. And she looked as if she was about to bat his hand away, but he slowed his touch.

"Just a moment," he said. "I promise I'm not going to do anything I shouldn't."

"You've already done several things that you shouldn't," she grumbled, but she waited, nibbling her soft lower lip.

He grinned again at her then, and slowly, carefully, he took a sprig of lavender from her hair and put it before her eyes. He twirled it ever so slightly.

"Oh," she said, her mouth forming a perfect circle of surprise.

"I was tempted to leave it there," he said.

"Why?" she demanded, her nose wrinkling.

Good God, he didn't know what was overcoming him, but he couldn't stop himself replying, "It looked rather perfect in your hair."

She let out a beleaguered sound. "Good Lord," she said. "You've been reading too many penny novelettes."

And with that, she turned on her booted heel again and marched through the fields. "Come along then, Mister..." She paused and called back over her shoulder, "And what is your name?"

"Mr. Summers."

She looked at him for a long moment and then let out another long sigh as if his name was as absurd as their meeting. Of course, it *was* absurd. He'd thought it up on his way here, though he'd given it little thought. It was the first name that came to mind as he'd been musing about his plans for the summer. But she couldn't know that.

"Very well, Mr. Summers," she said. "Come along. Let's get you where you belong."

This was not where he belonged. He belonged in London. But he was suddenly very glad that he had come here and into her field, even if only to stay for a short while.

Chapter Four

Alice had never had a man remove a flower from her hair. She'd also never been pulled to the ground in a lavender field before. And frankly, the entire day was a bit overwhelming. She considered herself to be a young woman of parts.

But she had not expected to find herself in a field with a man like…well, *this*. She had known that he was large when she approached him. As a matter of fact, that had been one of the things that had enraged her.

A large, bull-like man was in her field! Crushing her flowers! How dare he do such a thing? And so she had stridden up to him with what she thought were normal steps, but she must have been as quiet as a mouse. Or he'd been lost in reverie by the sight of her fields.

It happened often to her, if she was honest. But even so, she must have been ridiculously silent.

Because when she came upon him and exclaimed over his most unwanted trespass, he'd whipped around and nearly knocked her over. Much to his credit, he had grabbed her and then taken her down without crushing her beneath his formidable person.

This should have been alarming.

It was not. It had been pleasurable, which had been more alarming. His body, dear heaven, the strength of him had shocked her. And the feel of those muscles pressed up against her person! Shocking! In a strangely captivating way.

She had not known that the feelings she'd experienced existed. People had told her, of course. Many of the village girls did like to talk about kissing the village boys behind the barn doors, but she had kept herself well away from that.

She was never going to marry. That had been clear to her since she was ten years old. It had been impossible to miss the way her mother could barely do the tasks needed, let alone have room for dreams. She had seen her mother bear so many children, run the shop, and do everything she could to be a good wife.

And then she had been left alone, only to need to do more work. Whatever dreams her mother had? They'd died under the crushing weight of motherhood and family. And then widowhood.

No, she was not going to let her dreams, as her mother's were, be put aside, then broken. She was going to stay away from men, and so far, she had. She'd been very successful. But now she wondered if that success merely hinged upon the fact that she'd never met one that was as interesting as this fellow. No man had evoked such strong feelings within her before.

The scent of him was quite interesting. She'd noticed it right away.

It was very expensive. A stableman surely could not afford such a cologne. She was shocked because it was bergamot and citrus with a hint of spice that she was not quite aware of, and the base was beautiful. She knew most scents, but some were so exclusive, her mother could not obtain them. They came from distant shores, and so she was only aware of them through the descriptions in her mother's books.

When she drank it in, it sent shivers down her spine. Shivers that made her wish to lean in and inhale the notes along his strong neck. Of course, she had not! How could she? Such a thing was shocking.

The truth was, *he* was rather shocking. His expensive cologne was just the beginning.

To be fair, there was nothing cheap about this man, which gave her pause. Still, he'd said he was a new stable man, and she was taking him in the direction that he needed to go. She glanced back over her shoulder to make sure that the behemoth of a fellow was attending her.

He was quite close, his colossal body straining at his well-cut clothes as he moved along with surprising grace of movement.

And again, this felt rather alarming, and not, once again, because she was afraid of him, but because of the way he made her feel. He was well over six feet tall. His dark hair was longer than it should be, but perhaps he enjoyed the roguish look of what he thought a horse rider should look like.

No doubt Mr. Bilby would make him cut it. The land agent liked things to be run in a certain way.

She was very familiar with the few servants and the house at Helexton because she was required, as part of the rent, to work in their storage rooms and dry all of the herbs for the estate. It was quite a task every year to make certain that things were running as they should. When that time happened, which was quite soon, she was required to stay close to the main house, and she often took up rooms in the stables or with the ladies upstairs.

She did not like visiting the main house.

Like the villagers, those who worked in that house liked to whisper about her mother. It was something she didn't enjoy, hearing those suspicions. Her mother had warned her that people could be terrible. Sometimes, they still made suggestions that surely her mother in some way was a witch making poison potions.

It was ridiculous, of course.

There hadn't been witch trials in England in more than a hundred years, thank goodness, but people in these parts did still think that curses existed—and love potions.

Girls were always going to her mother, or even to Alice, asking for something, despite the fact that her mother was quite plain. She did not make things that could sway emotion. She did, however, make things that could smell very good, and that might attract a fellow.

It was clear to her that the fellow behind her was not wearing a love potion, but it did smell very good. She drew in a breath, and the scent wafted toward her, mixing with the salty air crashing in from the sea. As they headed toward the big house, she found herself wondering if she could go the entire way in silence and if he planned on doing so, too.

It was really probably the very best thing. But there was something odd about him that struck her as very curious. His clothes were finer than she assumed they should be for a stable hand, and that scent…

"Is it necessary to go so fast?"

"Am I going fast?" she asked without glancing back. She did not wish to see the breadth of his shoulders or the way his wasp waist descended into his perfect, dark breeches, or the fact that his legs looked like tree trunks. He was perfection under the sun.

It was annoying, all that perfection, because she *liked* it. And she did not want to like anything about a man. No. Men had their place, they were important, but she could not be distracted. She was going to go to London, and soon. Or so she told herself. She was saving as much money as she could, but it was no easy thing getting there.

She'd heard the stories. She'd read the novels about what happened to girls who went to London and did not have friends or mentors. It was terrible. They were often picked up by bawds or tricked into service, and then prostituted, or were abused by their masters.

So many young ladies met ruin in the city, and she refused to be ruined or wrecked. No, she was going to get her dream. She was going to get her dream for herself and her mother. Nothing was going to stop her.

And when they finally paused before the intimidating big house built of butter-yellow stone, she said to the man, "This is where you need to be. Would you like me to take you to the estate agent?"

"Yes, that would be very good," he said.

She gave a nod, let him lead the way, and climbed up the steps behind him.

But then…something quite odd happened. He stopped in front of the tall door and stared.

And for a moment, he continued to stand there in front of her, doing nothing.

She nearly ran into him. His shoulders were so large she could not see in front of him. Was there something there? Perplexed by his odd behavior, she inched around him to gaze at the door and its beautifully-made gold-plated handles

"May I ask what it is that you are doing?"

He blinked. "Whatever do you mean?"

She pointed to the door, and then to the golden latch, and said, "It's a handle. You press it, and then this happens." She pushed the door open, then tsked. "You are terribly rude, sir. You should have opened the door for me. Did no one teach you any sort of manners?"

He let out a strange gurgling sound. "My manners? Oh yes, they are most remiss. Forgive me."

Remiss, she thought to herself, and then she gasped. "Were you waiting for someone to open the door?"

"No," he said quickly.

Her eyes flared. "You *were* waiting for someone to open the door."

"No," he corrected, looking away. "I absolutely was not."

She let out a humorless laugh before she glared at him. "I don't think you are who you say you are, sir. And I'm sure it's none of my business, but—" She let out a gasp. "Are you certain this is where you are meaning to be? *You* are to run the stables? Are you…"

"What?" he queried her, his eyes narrowing as if he wished the whole subject would end.

She shook her head and pressed her hand to her temple. "No, no, I have read too many novels."

He quirked a brow, then teased, "I thought *I* was the one who'd read too many novels."

She cleared her throat. "Well, you are acting as if you're the long-lost son of a duke or something."

His eyes flared at that, and he looked so startled that she piped, "*Are* you the long-lost son of a duke? That would explain many things."

"What things would they explain?" he demanded, looking stunned.

"Well, for one, your cologne," she began. "A stable man would never wear that fine a scent. And you are not accustomed to opening your own doors, are you?"

He flinched.

"I am right!" She clapped her hands together, delighted but also quite flummoxed. "I did not realize I was such a detective. Why are you here? I hardly believe that it is to be a stable man. Have you come down in the world? Is it a scandal? Because really, we don't want scandal in this part of the world—"

"No," he cut in, looking quite chagrined. "Please stop talking."

She stared at him. "First you must tell me what the blazes are you all about?"

Then, much to her shock, he grabbed her hand and started tugging her back down the stairs and out toward the fields.

"Get your hands off me," she chastised, though she could not ignore the warm heat of his large, strong hand wrapped about hers.

"You like to say that, but I don't think you actually mean it. I've seen the way you were looking at me."

"How was I looking at you?" she scoffed, even as her heartbeat began to increase.

"As if you liked laying in the lavender field with me."

She scowled at him, rather annoyed that he was right. "Perhaps," she said, "but it's because I have never met anyone like you. You *don't* belong here."

"No," he agreed, clearly displeased to admit defeat, "I don't. And now I'm going to trust you with something."

She cocked her head to the side and gave him a wary glance. "I don't like secrets, and I don't like surprises."

"Perhaps you don't," he said, "but I am going to have to include you in on this because I'm clearly not as capable as I thought I was."

He let go of her hands and raised his own to show he meant no harm.

She folded her arms over her chest, which drew his eyes downward. Again.

"You, sir, are a rogue and a rake. Is that it?"

"No. Well, yes." He cleared his throat. "I am a rake. This is correct, but not in the capacity to which you think. It's simply part of what I'm supposed to do with my life."

"Who is supposed to be a rake as part of their life?"

she exclaimed. "Unless… Oh my goodness," she breathed, beginning to put all the pieces together. "Are you a lord?"

His throat worked as he swallowed. His entire face transformed as if he had been caught like a child at the sweets.

And then she began to back away. "Devil take it, this is far too complex, and I'm going to get myself into a great deal of trouble."

"You are not," he rumbled swiftly. "You are not going to get yourself into trouble at all. As a matter of fact, I think you can help me."

"Help you?" she echoed, doubting it very much.

"You're very astute," he said begrudgingly. "If I could, I would recruit you."

"Recruit me for what?" she queried. Was he mad? Perhaps he was an actor who had wandered off and suffered delusions of grandeur. She shook her head. "Never mind, I don't want to know—"

He drew in a long breath, which caused his beautiful, broad shoulders to settle into the most shockingly self-possessed posture she'd ever seen.

"I am the Earl of Enderley," he stated as if he did not need to elaborate much more. "I work at Horse Guards, and this is my estate."

She gaped at him, then began to inch backward. "Oh dear, *my lord*," she soothed. "Did you hit your head when you fell in the lavender field?"

He narrowed his eyes. "No," he said, and then he reached into his pocket.

"Whatever are you doing?"

"I assure you, you will not need to ask me to keep my hands off of anything again." And then he pulled out a signet ring. The falcon perched on an olive branch, and it was a stunning piece of artwork.

It was the same symbol that was above the estate doors.

She blinked, then gulped as it hit her. "You *are* the Earl of Enderley. Unless…of course…you've murdered him."

He let out an exasperated note. "I promise that I haven't murdered him, or anyone. Doesn't it make more sense that it is I, given the way I apparently smell and how I behave? I'm simply terrible at hiding my true self. At least from you."

She drew in a long breath, thinking, then concluded, "Yes, it does make sense, but why the devil would you come here and say you're to be the new stable man, especially since you clearly don't know how to act like one?"

"Well," he began, then said plainly, "I've heard that Mr. Bilby is an absolute ass."

She stared at him for a long moment, stunned that a gentleman of his position would care. "He is," she replied.

The earl smiled. "And so you're going to help me prove it."

Chapter Five

Life had always come easily to Felix.

It was part of being the son of an earl and then being an earl. When one was one of the ruling class of England, things simply unfolded before you. It didn't make it pleasant, but it certainly made it easy. He had been born with power and wealth.

He had been raised learning Greek as if it was his first language. He knew Homer, and he knew all of Europe, Russia, and parts of the continent of Africa.

He had skills that most people could never dream of having, because he had the access to those education systems. He could fight with a sword. He could ride a horse. He could hunt. He could speak five languages, French being only slightly behind his ancient Greek.

It was his exceptional fluency in French that had made him invaluable at Horse Guards. But in all of that time, he had never made so many mistakes so quickly as he had done with *her*. He had not realized his arrogance was so immense. He'd genuinely thought he could pretend to be a working-class person and get away with it.

He felt like a fool. He *was* a fool.

It was not a pleasant sensation that was traveling through him as he quickly attempted to decide what course to take next.

He was rather glad that it was she who had found out his foolery. But even so, there was a part of him that greatly disliked that he had let her down so entirely.

After all, she was a woman who, for entirely irrational reasons, he found he wished to impress.

"Attend me," he said, leading her further and further from the house, back toward the fields, lest they be spotted. "You have sussed me out rather quickly, but I do not think we should tell everyone who I actually am."

She frowned, her arms crossing just below her delectable bosom. "I'm still not entirely certain that I believe you're *the* earl."

He groaned. "Pick one of your fancies," he ground out. "You know that I'm not the master of stables. You're certain that I'm a gentleman, and I have shown you my signet ring."

"Yes," she relented, drawing in a deep breath. "All right. You're the Earl of Enderley." Her cheeks suddenly reddened. "I am speaking with an earl. It is very shocking. You realize I have never spoken with a titled person before."

"We drink water, eat food, and breathe air just as you do." He wished to set her at ease, even though her presence was doing anything but setting him at ease. No, quite the contrary. He could scarce tear his gaze away from her lush mouth or the curve of her body. Nor could he ignore how very much the way she spoke to him with such honesty made him feel both at sea and captivated.

A laugh tumbled past her lips, one that bespoke her annoyed amusement. "That is ridiculous. You don't do anything the same as we do."

Those lips... What he longed to do with them... He shook the thought quickly away, shoving his thoughts back to the moment at hand.

"Yes, we do," he countered, this time offended.

"No, you don't," she protested, her eyes flashing. "First of all, your water is poured from perfect crystal pitchers. Your food is the very best in all of the land, and the air that you breathe, well, it is always rarified. Is it not?"

"Have you been to London?" he drawled, thinking of the cloud of coal smoke that floated over the city.

At that, she hesitated, her face softening into an expression of keen longing before she replied, "No, I have not, though it is my dream to go."

"Your dream is to go to London?" The revelation shocked him as he looked about. "And leave this beautiful place? Good Lord, if I lived here, I would never leave."

She gave him a withering stare. "You clearly are not from here. You have never set foot here, and you have the privilege of going any place you want, whenever you want."

"That is not entirely true," he pointed out grimly. He wasn't about to go into a discourse of his duties and how the room he saw the most was his office at Horse Guards. "But I do take your point. Forgive me."

Then, as he considered the confession of her dreams, something took shape quickly in his mind. "But I have an idea."

"What is it?" she asked softly, warily.

"Your dream, it is to go to London."

"Well, not exactly," she said. "My dream is to go to London and study with Madame Clémence Dubois."

"The perfumer?" he clarified, amazed at her knowledge, which he supposed made him even more of an arrogant ass. What a lesson he was receiving today. "That is where I get my scent," he informed, rather pleased to make the connection.

It was quite strange, this connection. That he was wearing cologne made by the woman Miss Wright dreamed of studying with.

Her eyes rounded as she shifted on her booted feet and fidgeted. "Do you mind if I lean in and just…"

The very idea was both intimate and understandable if she wished to be a perfumer. Though reason said no, he said, "If you would like to…"

And with that, quite boldly, she leaned forward and drew in his scent very carefully. The action nearly caused him to abandon reason. Madness seemed quite common when around this woman, though he had been only in her company, one might argue, an hour.

She was driving him to the edge of desire in a way that no one had ever done before, and she wasn't doing anything that was particularly seductive. She pulled back then, slowly, and gazed up at him but wasn't really looking at him. She was going through some sort of mental catalog in her head.

"Bergamot and…citrus…" she murmured close to his throat before she drew back. "And a touch of something else. I will think of it. It will come to me, surely."

He wanted to pull her back toward his person to see if she smelled of sea salt, Cornish earth, and her lavender. He only barely refrained. "You are quite good. You must come to London," he said.

"Oh, just like that?" she scoffed impatiently. "Do you understand what it's like for a girl like me in London? I am not about to go and end up in some awful rooming house with a highwayman as my lover. Nor do I wish to die of the pox because a bawd got ahold of me."

He coughed. She was all but relaying the plot of a three-volume novel. "You do like to read, don't you?"

"What I am speaking of is also the subject of Hogarth's *A Harlot's Progress*," she replied scathingly. "I've seen the prints, and that was based upon his observations. And I will not end up in such a way. Now, we are wasting time, and someone could come at any moment."

"Then I will be quick," he said. "I want you to come to London, and I will set you up with Madame Clémence. I can make certain you have a place to stay. All of it, everything that you wish, will be supplied. I will introduce you to the right people. I shall make certain that you stay in a rooming house with other people who will not hurt you. I will check in on you and make certain that you are well."

. . .

Her arms began to slip to her sides at the host of his promises. It was almost cruel to have so much dangled before her. "Why should I trust you?"

"Well, that is a good question," he said honestly. "Perhaps you shouldn't. But I'm the only person who can give you your dreams."

She glared at him. "In exchange for what?" she asked, squaring her shoulders.

"You're going to help me ascertain whether or not Mr. Bilby is corrupt."

She goggled at him. Had she heard correctly? "I beg your pardon?"

"I don't think he's simply an ass," he said pointedly, his jaw tightening. "I think he's stealing funds from me."

"You have so many," she said, surprised he'd even made note of his missing pounds.

"Yes, but that's not the point. You're right. I don't need those funds," he said factually. "But those funds are meant to help people."

"What?" she queried. This was not at all what she expected. While he did not seem like a terrible fellow, now that she'd met him, everyone had thought the earl a right skin flint who didn't give two figs for the people who lived on his lands.

"They are meant to go toward new roofs, toward schools, toward the improvement of my lands, toward a vast many things," he said tightly.

"Oh," she said softly, suddenly beginning to understand him a bit better, beginning to think highly of him if he was honest. "You wish to do those kinds of things here?"

He nodded.

"Well, no one thinks so," she said quickly. "You're not seen as a good landlord. You're seen as an absent one."

He let out a groan. "Yes, that's what I feared, and I came down to see for myself. I don't think you should judge a man based off of accounts, so I want to talk to my tenants, but I don't want them to feel the pressure of having to talk to an earl. I want them to feel like they can speak to a man who is like them."

"You are nothing like them," she pointed out.

"Yes, you've made that clear. But you could help me be," he urged. "And I think that I can do it. I simply made a few mistakes with my ruse."

Her lips twitched. A few mistakes? He'd given himself away to her within minutes. Granted not many would make note of his cologne, but the way he approached the door was quite obvious. "You are very optimistic."

"It is the best way to stay alive," he said.

"Optimism?" she challenged.

"Oh yes," he affirmed. "If one chooses negativity, it is a slow, awful path."

"You mean it," she said, her eyes searching over his face. Was he truly so hopeful?

"Indeed, I do," he said. "With every bit of my soul."

She swallowed, hardly daring to believe that this was

happening.

Had the answer to her dreams truly, suddenly popped up in her lavender field this day?

She cleared her throat and clarified, "You will take me to London, you will set me up not in your house as a mistress or some nefarious thing, but in a place, in a rooming house with girls, and you'll make certain that I have an opportunity to work at the perfumery?"

"I promise," he said.

And he said it so simply and with such utter sincerity it stole her breath away.

She forced herself to reply, "I don't know if I can believe you."

"Perhaps you don't, but I can have letters drawn up and information sent from my solicitors, if that makes you feel any better. I can also write to Madame Clémence and ask for a position for you. You will hear within the week."

She gazed at him, her mouth dropping open. "It isn't possible," she said. Tears stung her eyes. It would be so cruel, if it did not come true…now that it was dangling before her.

He leaned forward, narrowing the great distance between their heights, and in his deliciously deep voice, he rumbled, "That your dreams might actually come true?"

Her mouth snapped shut at that, and then she realized that's exactly what it was. Her heart all but skipped a beat.

She had been clinging to hope for years, but deep in her heart, she'd never really believed it could happen.

And here, on a whim, a chance meeting, he was going to make it happen.

"Will you help me, Miss Wright?" he asked.

And then, much to her shock, she stuck a hand out between them and said, "I will."

He slipped his own hand about hers. His palm swallowed it up.

And there near the fields she loved so well, she made a deal.

She only prayed that it was the right thing to do. If things didn't go well with Mr. Bilby, if he found a way to punish Alice and her mother for this investigation, and the earl didn't make good on the promise he just made, she'd be in a much worse situation than she was even now.

Chapter Six

Alice had never experienced such a strange day in all her life. Of course, there had been the day that the two-headed goat had been born a county over. And then there had been the time the school mistress had run off with the vicar.

But the Earl of Enderley and all that came with him was unbeatable.

And as she realized how her life might entirely change, she wondered something.

"How on earth did you get this job?" she blurted.

A chagrined look crossed his face. "I hired myself," he admitted.

She let out a low groan that was half laugh. "Of course you did."

"What?" He shrugged. "I have the experience to do it."

"No, you don't," she returned, amazed at his audacity. "You're probably good with horses. And that is all."

"I am excellent with horses." He waggled his brows. "I can pick the finest horse at Newmarket. Every race."

"That is not the same as running a stable," she pointed

out, exasperated by his confidence.

"Perhaps not," he agreed, "but I do know how to muck one out, I promise you that."

"Oh, I'm so glad to hear it," she said and pointed toward Helexton House. "But you can't go into that house right now and meet Bilby. You can't even go to the stables right now."

He frowned, clearly thinking far more of his abilities than she did. Being an earl likely did that to one.

"Why not?" he demanded.

She all but gaped at him. "Because you're clearly not prepared."

Then to her surprise, instead of arguing, he asked, "What do you suggest?"

She thought for a moment. "Are you expected today?"

"Later this afternoon," he said. "It's why I was on foot. I felt I had time."

"I see," she mused before an idea hit her and she seized upon it. "You're going to come home with me."

"I beg your pardon?"

"You're going to come to my shop where we live." The plan began formulating in her head, just like the new recipe for a perfume. "You're going to compose a letter from the earl saying that you, *Mr. Summers*, are going to take rooms in my mother's house, that you're a very special person who knows horses particularly well, and any desire you have is to be indulged. You must say you don't particularly like to live in a stable block and you have arranged a room."

He blinked, his eyes darkening and not with displeasure. "You want me to live with you?"

"Yes," she began, "I want you to live with me because you are going to get yourself in so much trouble within moments if you live near other servants. You clearly have no idea what you are doing. How is it possible that you work at Horse Guards?" she asked, hardly believing it.

She had read about Horse Guards, and she did know that it was largely about running the military, and she was guessing there was some intrigue involved with him.

"You're not a spy, are you?" she whispered, her stomach tightening.

"No, I am most certainly not a spy," he said. "I am too tall to be a spy."

She shook her head. "Too tall? What do you mean?"

"Exactly what I said," he returned. "People of my height? It's not possible for us to be spies."

She frowned.

He gestured up and down his rather intense and captivating limbs to help her understand. "I stand out. No matter how hard I tried, and I *did* try, I will tell you it is impossible for me to hide easily in a crowd."

"How tall are you?" she asked.

"How tall do you think I am?" he teased.

She pursed her lips and picked a number. "Clearly over six feet."

"I am six foot three," he groaned. "It is a blessing and a curse, but I can't hide in small spaces. So, for instance, if someone needed to shove me into a hidey-hole, I wouldn't be able to fit."

"Oh my," she said, biting back a laugh, for it clearly mattered to him. But then she wondered...was he so very large *everywhere*?

She shoved the naughty and scandalous thought away before it could blossom. As it was, her skin was already tingling at the idea.

"So you have no field experience pretending to be someone that you're not. Is that what I understand?"

"Correct."

"Well, that makes all of this more understandable," she relented and found herself rather relieved. As a matter of fact, a good deal of tension left her shoulders. "Now, you are going to come home with me, and we are going to train you so that you can do the work that you wish, or you can simply go fire Bilby now. No one likes him."

He thrust a hand through his hair. "I can't fire a man because no one likes him," he said, "and I want to know what exactly is going on, which will take a bit of time. You see, I need to know if the man should be jailed."

"Jailed?" she whispered.

"Yes," he said tightly. "For fraud."

"My goodness." She was scarce able to draw breath. "You're very serious."

His visage turned austere. It was so handsome, so roguish, but suddenly, it was a hard plane of determination. "I'm a man of honor, if I'm honest with you."

She swallowed, rather overwhelmed by his strength and his apparent honor in that moment. "Well, that's good to hear, considering our arrangement. Now, come along."

And with that, she darted further along the road that led away from the house.

They had to go as quickly as possible, because the truth was, he would not last long. If he had forgotten about stopping in front of a door and opening it himself, the man was going to be an absolute disaster and Bilby would call him out. Maybe even fire him. She had to suppress a laugh at the thought of Bilby firing the earl from his own estate. They crossed the fields quickly and headed to the small house that was on the edge of the village.

It was a hodgepodge abode, but it was *hers*.

She adored her family's home. It had been in existence for more than four hundred years and was slightly crooked. She loved the fact that the house was a bit tilted, as if it was quite tired and was not able to stand any longer yet refused to give up its dignity. There was a sign above the door, indicating that it was a place to get cures for ailments.

She quickly opened the door, and the bell rang overhead.

Her mother let out an exclamation. "You're home early, my dear. Is something amiss?"

"Oh, Mama, you have no idea what sort of adventure I've had today. I'd like to introduce you to someone. This is the—"

He coughed loudly.

"Uh, this is Mr. Summers," Alice said swiftly.

"How do you do, Mr. Summers?" her mother said, bouncing the littlest, who was not four years of age, on her hip. Oliver laughed and tried to grab for his mother's hair.

"He is the new stableman," Alice said swiftly, hoping to get him upstairs. Her mother was observant but tired. And her never-ending work looking after her children and the shop rendered her distracted. "He is going to run the stables at the big house."

"Oh, how wonderful," her mother gushed. "I do like horses."

She blinked. She'd had no idea. "You do, Mama?"

"Yes, my dear." A light filled her mother's eyes as a memory danced there. "When I was quite young, I used to love to ride, but when I began having children, there was simply never any time."

She often forgot that her mother had had a whole other life in France. She had been raised there but came over as a child, losing her accent.

"Well, Mama," she said, "we are to give him a room."

Her mother gaped. "I beg your pardon? But how will he survive the children?"

"The earl wishes him to stay with us," she explained, steeling herself to her falsehood, though she hated it. "You are always saying how a lodger would be just the thing, and he will rent a room."

"I promise, I will not mind the young ones," the earl

assured. "I am used to an unruly house."

She wondered if he had any idea how unruly a house of six could be. But they would soon find out.

Her mother's face warmed with relief. "Oh, how wonderful. We can use the extra income. Alice's brother is hoping to go to college."

"That's wonderful," the earl declared sincerely. "And what is he going to study? I can help him with his Greek."

"No, you can't!" Alice hissed, almost stomping on his boot. The man was a walking disaster. It was clearly not just his height that prevented him from being an actual spy.

"Imagine," her mother trilled, but then she frowned, her brow furrowing as she began to realize how odd that was, "a stableman who speaks Greek. However did you learn?"

The earl audibly swallowed and then rushed, "My father was a schoolmaster."

"Oh, that makes sense," her mother said, pleased at the explanation. "Your accent is quite interesting. You are clearly not from these parts. It does sound as if you went to Oxford."

"I did," he said softly.

How the blazes would she get him to stop? She wasn't certain. But surely, he realized he was digging himself a hole?

"Oh, how lucky you are," her mother returned. "You must tell us how you managed it financially. It is most difficult, but my son, Robert, he's so clever, and I really think he could have a chance."

"I'd be happy to help him," the earl said, as though it was the easiest thing in the world.

Alice swung her gaze back and forth from her mother to the earl and had no idea what to say. She only prayed the earl was not jesting, because if he was, it would break his mother's heart.

"Now, Mother," Alice interjected, desperate to get him away. "I'm going to show him upstairs. Are the other children out?"

"Yes. Thank goodness," her mother said with a smile. "They have all run to buy sweets over at Mrs. Smith's shop."

"Oh, good. They'll be out for a bit, then." She did not wish the earl to have to be tossed in the fire too soon.

Then, unable to bear the potential for her mother to also deduce that Mr. Summers was actually the Earl of Enderley, she did something rather rash. She reached back and took his hand and began pulling him up the stairs.

She felt her mother's eyes upon her, and she chose to ignore it. It was an unusual state of affairs. She knew it, but sometimes life called for unusual measures.

As soon as they were upstairs, Alice opened a door and thrust him through. "My goodness. You speak Greek?" she exclaimed.

"I could have opened this door myself," he pointed out. "I do know how to learn."

She crossed to the bed and began pulling the bedclothes off. She'd have to get fresh linen. "Well, I'm glad. Clearly, you can if you went to Oxford. Did you go to Eaton, too?"

"No." His lips twitched. "Harrow."

She let out a sigh. "God help us."

"In my experience," he said, "God prefers people who help themselves."

She punched at the pillow and considered strangling it. "You're going to be very difficult, aren't you?"

"I have been told so in the past," he agreed with undue cheer, "but I do my best to be helpful."

She whirled around and pinned him with a hard stare. "You best keep up your promise to my mother about Robert."

"Oh, I will. I'm sure I shall have time. How difficult can running a stable be? And I cannot pursue Bilby's interactions all day. I shall make time for your brother."

She closed her eyes and was tempted to throw herself

down upon the bed and simply hope she was dreaming. Was he truly real? Surely not. "You didn't just say that, did you? About the difficulties of a stable?"

He frowned. "I'm being privileged again, aren't I?"

"Yes, you are," she said, not sure if she wanted to shake him or embrace him for both his thoughtlessness around work and his kindness to her family. "But that is, I suppose, to be expected. I can't blame you for how you were raised." She strode toward him then, taking note of his clothes and stance. "Now, everything about you is wrong."

"What do you mean?" he protested.

"Your clothes? They're cut too well. We need to rough you up a bit. Your accent... It is too perfect. And," she said, gesturing at him, as if the entirety of his person was a difficulty, "stablemen don't speak Greek."

"Well, they do if their father's a teacher," he countered smugly.

"All right," she said, determined to drive her point home. "Where did your father teach?"

"Oh, I see." He folded his hands behind his back. "I shall come up with a believable backstory this evening. Knowing you has helped me gain perspective on what I need to do." He shrugged. "All shall be well."

All shall be well. It was a nice saying, but she couldn't agree.

In her experience, life was full of pitfalls.

"Well, I'm going to buy you a few things," she said.

"You don't have to do that, Miss Wright."

"Oh, I do," she said, refusing to brook argument. "I most certainly do. We must make you look like a man who tames horses, who rides them, and who takes care of thoroughbreds. Do not get yourself into trouble, and when we are done, I shall take you out to the estates."

He smiled. "That sounds ideal."

And with that, she backed out of the room quickly and closed the door, leaving him inside. Her life had been turned upside down in a whirlwind.

She raced back downstairs.

"My dear," her mother called from behind the counter, holding Oliver on her hip, trying to feed him porridge and also do the accounts, "that was most odd."

"Yes, Mama," she agreed. Her pulse began to increase, and she felt her cheeks heat. She did not like lying to her mother. "He is odd, isn't he?"

"Very," she said. "He's a stableman? He doesn't even have the scent of horses about him."

Of course her mother would notice something like that. She gave a nervous laugh. "He must love bathing."

"But his cologne…" her mother mused.

"Yes, yes. Isn't it delightful?" she rushed, eager to get away from her mother's well-meaning interrogation.

"It's far too expensive, my dear," her mother pointed out. "I wonder who gifted it to him. Perhaps his last employer."

"Yes, Mama," she said, hating the feel of her own subterfuge. She'd never lied to her mother before, not even for a good cause. "How clever you are. It must have been his last employer."

Alice turned, heading towards the doorway.

"Where are you going?"

"Oh, just to buy a few things."

Her mother blanched. "My dear, we don't have any extra money."

"Oh, they're not for me," she explained.

"Who are they for?"

Alice pointed upward.

"Mr. Summers?"

"Yes. He has no clothes. They got lost on the way here, and he wants to make sure he makes a good impression on

Mr. Bilby."

Her mother cocked her head to the side, causing her dark hair, which was laced with silver, to shine in the afternoon light. "He's dressed very finely, my dear."

"Yes, but it's not appropriate wear, is it, for riding horses and taking care of them?"

"Well, no, that is most definitely true," her mother said, and since she was always tired and always busy, she gave a nod, letting the whole matter go. "How very kind of you, my dear. You must be off."

It was always the case. She dearly loved her mother. But she did not have the strength or time to truly pay attention to Alice's comings and goings.

How very kind of you, she'd said.

"Kind" wasn't the right word.

Manipulative, yes. That was the word.

She truly loathed keeping the truth from her loving mama, but this was her chance at her dreams, and she was not going to throw it away.

Chapter Seven

"Would you like to address the way I walk, as well?" Felix drawled. After all, Alice had addressed just about everything else about him in the last two hours.

"No," she said. "We don't have time, number one. And number two, I rather like the way you walk."

That sent a wave of pleasure through him. As they strode back across the road heading out to his estate, he asked, "You do, do you?"

"Yes, I do," she replied, keeping her gaze firmly ahead. "There's something rather roguish about it. You walk around the world as if you own it all, which I think a man who's very good with horses might do." Then she gave him a look, which was quite mischievous. "But I am not entirely certain."

"Do I really?" he asked, taking those words in, his stomach tightening.

"Do you what?" she queried.

"Walk about as if I own the world."

She let out a snort of a laugh. "You didn't know?"

"No, I didn't know," he admitted, dismayed. "There's

apparently a vast many things about myself that I don't know."

Her violet gaze turned upon him, sparking with interest. "You go through the world as if everyone should simply get out of your way. You're not rude. My mother thought you were rather lovely, actually."

"Your mother is lovely," he countered, thinking on how the woman showed such love to all her children. "It is clear how hard she works, and yet she was gracious to me without any need to be."

"You offered to teach my brother Greek!" she teased.

"Yes, but that is not why she was kind," he replied, certain of this and quite moved. Mrs. Wright was kind down to the tips of her toes, and he admired that very much.

And as they approached the estate, he spotted a man walking toward them. His hair was white, his paunch was large, and his shoulders sagged.

There was an angry nature to his stance.

"Oh, bloody hell," he said under his breath, his body tensing. "That's him, isn't it?"

"Bilby?" she piped, eyeing the man coming toward him. "Yes, it is."

"Are we late?" he asked, tempted to pull his pocket watch but remembering a man of his status could never afford to own the one he had.

"No, I don't think so."

He fought a scowl. Even he knew meeting his future *employer* with a dark countenance wasn't wise. "He looks very displeased."

"It's his general nature," she replied tartly.

"Ah," he surmised, readying himself to interact with the lemon of a human. "So he's a terrible land agent and sour."

"Yes," she replied.

"Hello," Felix called. "Are you Mr. Bilby?"

Bilby eyed him up and down like he wanted to chuck him

out to sea, but he would never be capable of such a task. The man was old and looked quite cantankerous.

Felix thrust out his hand, trying to take on the custom that Miss Wright had taught him. "How do you do? I am Mr. Summers."

"Mr. Summers," Mr. Bilby said with a curl of his lips. "I do not like this at all."

"You don't?" he queried, attempting to feign surprise. The man's displeasure was as evident as the nearness of the sea.

"No," Bilby gritted, tugging at his expensive, silk waistcoat. "I am in the habit of hiring people on this estate. Now, I understand the earl chose you personally, but I want you to know that I shall be watching you to make sure that you do a good job. Those horses are worth a fortune, and I will not have you harm a single one."

"I welcome the criticism," Felix replied evenly. "I would hate for anything to happen to the horses."

And he did his very best to modulate his tone, to drop it, to make his voice more lilting. A country air, so to speak, rather than an upper-class drawl.

Bilby sniffed. "You have a room in the stables. It's not large. Your bed is made of straw. It will do, though."

And suddenly, Felix began to wonder if Bilby was hoping to drive him away. Maybe he didn't want someone that the earl had appointed personally. After all, if the earl wasn't here, it was Bilby's own little kingdom, wasn't it?

His hands longed to curl into fists, and it was all he could do to keep his face a mask of calm.

This was all very interesting.

"I am not going to be staying there," Felix said, rather enjoying the fact he could at least wind the man up to some degree without revealing himself.

"What the devil you talking about?" Bilby ground out.

"Of course you are. How can you run the stables without living in them?"

"Do you live in the Great House?"

Bilby tensed. "I do not. Don't be absurd."

"But you run the estate," Felix returned, leading him along.

Bilby's eyes narrowed, and Miss Wright cleared her throat. Felix realized that he was on dangerous ground. Men like Summers did not question their betters. That was something she had said.

It was going to be difficult to keep to.

"Ah, forgive me," Felix began pleasantly, pivoting quickly. "I'm merely pointing out that the earl"—he produced the letter that he had written but an hour earlier—"wishes me to room with Miss Wright and her mother."

"Why in God's name would he wish you to dwell with them?" Bilby snapped. "They are quite odd."

Felix shrugged, doing his best to look as puzzled by the events as Bilby was. "Who knows with an earl and his whims?"

Bilby blew out his breath. "Come along, then. Let's introduce you to the horses. You don't need Miss Wright any longer."

"I suppose I don't." Felix let a slow smile tilt his lips, thinking up a reason on the spot to keep Alice in their company. "Only I did promise her that I would introduce her to a horse."

Alice's eyes widened, but she quickly composed herself. He hoped she understood he simply needed her around to make sure he didn't fumble up his ruse.

"Do what with a horse?" Bilby said as if it was the most ridiculous idea he'd ever heard. "You can do that on your own time."

"It would be convenient if we were to all go together

now, don't you think?" he suggested, refusing to give in but making sure to sound damn pleasant about it.

Bilby rolled his eyes and then turned his gaze to Alice, scrutinizing, then concluding her company wouldn't be so very terrible. "Fine, then, come along."

With that, he began marching off toward the paddocks and stables. They should have been finer and better kept. It was the one thing he noticed immediately. He loved horses, and he had assumed that the horses he sent down to the country were being well taken care of.

Bilby extended his hand. "You see? Look at all this beautiful green pasture. We send the horses out all the time."

Felix paused as anger began to pulse through him. And he could not stop himself as he assessed, "Some of the fences don't look like they're in particularly good repair. And there are definitely large divots in the ground. Thoroughbreds can break their legs easily on an uneven field."

Bilby pursed his lips. "Well, clearly you'll have your work cut out for you, then. I should let you get straight to it. Make sure everything is as his lordship would like. I have things to do."

Clearly not wishing to hear another word on the subject, Bilby turned and walked away.

"Good Lord," Felix said once the man was out of earshot. "What an experience that was. I've met men like him in London. Sour little people who love to beat little boys who won't go up chimneys." Felix tensed, a new thought occurring to him. "Has he abused children here?"

Alice winced. "The village school, which is on your land, is not very good. He hired a schoolmaster who does love to beat the children."

He blew out of breath as his anger churned to wrath in his guts. "Dear God, I should just tell them who I am right now so I can get rid of him. But I need to collect more information first, because I don't want him to be able to go on to the next estate and do the exact same thing there."

Her brows rose. "Oh, I see. You're playing a long game and trying to help as many as you can."

"Yes, precisely." His shoulders dropped. He found himself surprisingly relieved that she understood what he was trying to do and that it wasn't just a silly whim.

"Come along," he said. "Let's go meet the horses."

Her face brightened. "You were serious about introducing me?"

"Quite," he said. "I had a feeling you would love it."

She followed eagerly, as if she was being swept up in all of this, too.

As they strode into the stables, he saw several young boys cleaning out a stall. "Where are the other stable hands?" he asked them.

"We're it, sir," said a redhead, who appeared to be the eldest.

"You three?" he asked, stunned. His anger still simmered inside him from Bilby, but he did not wish the boys to feel it. "None of you look more than twelve years old."

"They're cheap," Alice whispered.

"Ah, yes, that makes sense," he said. "And they're doing an excellent job considering."

He forced himself to say it, for he had no wish to offend the boys.

But this was appalling.

Twelve-year-old boys, no matter how capable, could not manage thoroughbreds. While it was true that the smaller the rider, the better the jockey, they were not jockeys. They were not meant to race the horses. They were meant to take care of them. And thoroughbreds were large animals, high strung, and sometimes could hurt other people or themselves or each other.

They needed a strong, steady, gentle hand.

"We'll get this sorted out," he stated, willing himself to good cheer for their sakes. "I am Mr. Summers, and you are?"

The oldest one introduced himself. He had curling red hair. "I'm Tom," he said. "This is George."

George had black hair that stuck up at strange angles.

"And this is Michael," Tom finished.

Michael was blond. His hair was rather long, and his eyes were a riveting shade of blue.

None of them were dressed well or looked as if they ate enough.

"Do you know Miss Wright?" he ventured.

Tom grinned. "We've all seen her, but we've not had the pleasure of making her acquaintance."

"How do you do, Miss Wright?" George said with a wary smile.

They all pulled their forelocks at her.

"How do you do?" she returned.

"How are the horses?" Felix asked, dreading the reply.

"As well as horses could be expected," Tom said carefully, though he did not look as if he entirely believed what he said. In fact, he looked terrified he was about to get in trouble.

"Are they getting their proper exercise?" Felix asked, even as dread began to wash through him.

The boys stared at him

"Have none of you worked with thoroughbreds before?"

Tom shifted. "No, sir. You're not going to fire us, are you? We earn a small income here to take home to our mothers."

A muscle tightened in his jaw. Hiring boys for the stable was good. They should be here and paid well, but they needed guidance. "No, I'm not going to fire you, lad. I'm sure you're very capable of learning what needs to be done."

The boy blew out a harsh breath.

He was going to murder Bilby once he had all his

information collected. Perhaps a magistrate wasn't necessary after all.

He could do the job himself.

"Come along, then," he called, drawing himself up. All of this might be far worse than even he'd expected.

He went down the stables, listening.

There was a horse dancing out of agitation.

He could hear the thumps and noises of distress all the way from here.

The animal was banging at the stall.

"What's wrong with that one?" he asked gently.

"Wayward?" Tom asked, looking afraid of the big animal. "He's always out of sorts."

"Who rides him?" Felix asked, hardly daring to believe it was so bad as this.

"No one." George kicked at the straw on the ground as he dared to admit, "None of us are capable."

"Of course not you," he said, his voice tight. "That's not your job. Doesn't Bilby bring in riders?"

The boys all shook their heads.

His hands folded into fists. For a steadying moment, he closed his eyes. He couldn't allow his anger to build to rage. It would do no good here.

He crossed to the closed stable and saw the beautiful silver stallion. He was massive. Seventeen hands. The fellow looked like he could do a mile in no time. He'd be a treasure at market soon. But he was young and clearly angry at being kept penned up.

"Here, lovely boy. Here," he said, nickering to the horse, holding out his hand, soothing.

The horse's withers trembled, his eyes flicked back and forth. His ears turned this way and that. He was full of pent-up energy and frustration.

Felix wanted to go and grab Bilby and throttle him, but

such energy would do no good around an animal.

"All of you," he said gently. "Take a few steps back and think of something lovely."

"Think of something lovely?" Miss Wright blurted. "Why—"

"Horses are very intuitive creatures," he said, keeping his voice a gentle sing-song. "They can tell if you're angry or afraid. And it will not make their temperament any better. In fact, they will act out and not trust you."

Tom frowned. "You're serious, Mr. Summers."

"I am, boy," he returned, all the while keeping his eyes on Wayward. "Think of apples. Think of cake. Think of cherries. It doesn't matter what. Think of your mother if you like her, but you must be calm around a beast like this. They're very sensitive."

And then Felix opened the stable door and slipped inside.

Chapter Eight

Alice had read about poetry in motion, but she'd never actually understood the concept until she'd seen the earl ride a horse.

He was like a god.

'Twas as if a mythic figure from the stories of old had come down from the sky and was now amongst them. It was elemental. Powerful. Beautiful.

He sat balanced as if he'd been born to do it. His strong body rode easily. His hands gently held the reins. And she felt certain that in this part of his ruse, he would need no help at all. He would not need a saddle. He would not need reins. He was simply one with the animal.

The stallion raced about the paddock, wildly charging, his body a song of pure perfection as it stretched out its legs and ate up the earth with its hooves.

Watching was magic. And she felt swept up in something pure.

He was perfection. His long dust coat flew out behind him, and his shoulders were a work of art as he easily maneuvered the beast. It looked as if he was doing nothing.

And yet she knew it was not nothing to be at one with such a massive animal.

Mr. Summers…the Earl of Enderley…he was steering the stallion as if through the barest touch or whisper, he could speak the horse's language.

The awe at them together nearly undid her. And there was also the fact that just moments before, the animal had been close to rage, furious at its captivity and being treated so poorly.

She wanted to kick herself.

Was this estate *entirely* full of such things?

Boys who were not taken care of, animals who were penned up. She knew about the schoolmaster, and of course, houses that were not fit to live in.

How could that be a fit life? It was not life at all!

No, this was life. The man upon the stallion who was racing around the paddock as if life was art and nothing could stop the flow of it? He had come here to stop Bilby, and she was beginning to think that this actually was what life was about.

Poetry in motion and cruelty ended.

The earl stopped the stallion but feet away from the boys and herself. He stroked the animal's shoulder. "What a good lad," he said, his voice a soft purr.

The sound of that voice, rich and rumbling, traveled through her, and she fought a gasp. Again, he kept surprising her. All her life, she'd never been particularly intrigued by gentlemen. But he intrigued her.

The earl turned his dark gaze to her. He seemed completely alive, crackling with vitality now that he'd been out with the stallion.

"Come," he urged, offering his hand to her.

"What?" She almost took a step back. "No."

"I promised I'd introduce you," he said with a slow smile.

She straightened her spine, refusing to show that she was intimidated by so much life and power. "You may do so at this distance. We shall be proper about it."

"Proper?" he teased. "There's nothing proper about a thoroughbred stallion. They are all muscle, and they are ready to run."

"I don't think it's a very good idea," she hedged.

He cocked his head to the side. "He's perfectly gentle now. He and I understand each other. Well, not gentle, exactly. He'll have his quirks, but I promise you'll be safe."

"Do not make promises you cannot keep," she warned.

He leaned forward slightly, his dark hair tumbling about his shoulders. And there was a shadow now along his jaw, which did exactly what she'd hoped it would do when she told him not to shave. Since they had met that morning, he'd already grown quite a shadow. And it gave him a slightly less aristocratic demeanor.

He did look like a roguish horseman with that dark stubble. Someone who knew horseflesh better than all the others.

"I thought you were one for adventure," he challenged.

She let out a note of protest at that. "How dare you?" she said with faux outrage. "Throw my dreams in my face. Wishing to be a perfumer is an entirely different thing than getting up on an animal like that."

"Not really," he returned, stroking his hand along the horse's neck. The stallion dropped its head, its long lashes soft and lids fluttering half closed. "It's all a chance."

She sucked in a slow breath. "Fine then. If you wish it."

And so she tucked her hand into his.

"Surely," she said, looking about, "there needs to be a stable block."

But before she could spot one, he was hauling her up, easily swinging her onto Wayward.

"Hold tight," he called, swinging her up in front of him.

"Never you fear. I've got you."

He wrapped his arms about her, and then they were off.

At first, she hated it. She wanted to let out a scream of protest. The wild gait of the horse was most unruly and terribly uncomfortable. But then she focused on *him*, focused on the way his arms were wrapped about her, focused on the way that she knew she could never fall. His hard chest was pressed to her back. She could feel the muscles of his thighs making certain that she could not tumble either way.

The earl was completely at ease. There wasn't a single bit of tension to his body. This was bliss to him.

His gloved hands easily shifted the reins, just tapping the leather lightly, gently on the horse's neck, and the animal seemed to know exactly what was required.

The next thing she knew, they were out of the paddock, racing across the fields.

"What are we doing?" She gasped, her heart in her mouth, for she had never gone so quickly upon a horse. People like herself rarely rode for she had no funds to keep a horse.

"We are having an adventure," he said.

And they raced along. It felt like flying. There was no other word for it. They passed the three boys, whooping and hollering, crying out excitedly. And then they were all the way down the field, far away from the children.

She felt the surge and power of the beast below her, rocking underneath her hips. She could scarce catch her breath. It was exhilarating, and she had never felt so alive as she did in this moment.

She had not realized that her entire life had been about getting up, working, then going to bed. Oh, there were small pleasures, of course, laughing with her mother and her brothers and sisters, her work with her flowers, turning such things into perfumes.

But this was something entirely different.

Here, with the earl, upon Wayward, she could not think of the past. She could not think of the future. She could only think of this blissful moment atop this beast whose body shook and moved as if it were the earth beneath her.

And then he gently pulled the stallion to a slow walk, and Wayward lowered his head and happily ate at the grass, an entirely different beast now.

She laughed, shaking as she leaned back against him.

"You liked it, didn't you?"

"I did," she confessed, her body all but buzzing with the excitement of it.

"Yes," he said softly. "You are a creature for adventure."

"I'm glad you think so," she replied. "But if it's all like this, who wouldn't wish adventure?"

"It's not all like this," he admitted. "You never know what could be around the corner. Luckily, we've got to him in time."

"What do you mean?" she queried.

"Just like a human." His voice reverberated in his chest, the hum of it teasing her as he continued. "If one treats an animal badly for long enough, they will internalize all of that, and they will strike out in anger and do harsh things."

"Are you suggesting Mr. Bilby—"

"I don't know Bilby's history," he cut in. "But given his behavior, he probably had a horrible childhood. That doesn't mean he has the right to do what he's doing to others. Not to this beast, not to the children at the school."

He was silent for a long moment before he placed his gloved hand over hers. "Thank you for helping me," he said.

She licked her lips, the feel of his hand resting on hers a revelation. "I haven't helped you at all yet."

"You have," he insisted. "And you are going to help me more, aren't you?" His voice was a soft whisper along her neck.

She nodded against his shoulder, her entire body

crackling with the thrill of being so close to him. "You're a fast learner."

"Thank you," he said. "In truth, I do the teaching at Horse Guards. I think I'm better at being a teacher than doing the thing."

"Many teachers are," she said gently.

"Do you think so?"

She drew in a long breath, trying to contain the way she felt with him. The hum of something she couldn't quite describe emanating from her core, pulsing through her veins.

She shoved it aside. She had to. She couldn't allow it. So she turned her thoughts to safe things. Things that would make her recall her purpose.

"My mother..." she began, shocked as she dared to share her own story with him. "She's a wonderful teacher, but she never got to fulfill her dreams. She never got to be a perfumer."

"You're going to fulfill them for both of you," he breathed.

"With your help, yes."

They were silent for several agonizing moments. For in the silence, she could not deny the intensity between them, growing slowly, powerfully.

But this feeling between them, it was too much. It was undeniable. She cleared her throat, fighting with all her might.

"Where are we to go next? Surely you wish to begin your research."

"Where do you suggest?" he asked, letting the stallion walk, and the roll of the horse's gait caused their bodies to undulate together.

"Visiting Mr. Perkins," she rushed, shocked how her voice was low and soft. "You should see his house and the state it's in."

"And the account books?" he queried. "Have you ever seen them?"

"In the house?" she asked, frowning. This question filled her with dread. This was going to be far harder than she'd hoped. "No, I've not seen the books, but I do go into the house to work in the herb kitchens."

"Wonderful," he replied. "Can you think of a scenario to get me inside? Otherwise, I won't be able to. I'll have to sneak in at night. And that has its own set of risks."

"Yes," she said at last, daring. Daring to do what was necessary for her dreams. "I can think of something to get you inside."

Alice tilted her face back toward his, and she froze. He was looking down at her. There was something mysterious and dark in his gaze, something hungry as he watched her. His arms tightened about her ever so slightly, and he lifted his gloved hand to her cheek.

"You're very brave, aren't you? You've endured quite a lot, and still you're making a success of it."

"I'm doing the best I can," she whispered, emotion welling deep within her.

His mouth parted slightly, and for a shocking moment, she was certain that he was going to kiss her. And for an even more shocking moment, she was absolutely certain that she wanted him to.

She broke the moment and pulled away. "I think you should take me back," she said stiffly. "Let's talk to the boys and see what they know."

His throat worked as he swallowed.

But he did exactly as she said, gently urging the horse forward, who picked up speed and crossed the paddock again as if it was nothing.

The sensation of flying returned, but she knew that she had ended the thrill of it, shoved it aside. There was too much at stake to give into such thrills, and she would not let herself yield.

Chapter Nine

He'd made more mistakes in the last few days with her than he had made in his entire life.

The horse ride, that had not been a mistake, but the way he had leaned down, longing to devour her mouth with his own?

That had been a mistake.

He did not know what had overtaken him. He was usually a man of control. After all, men like him were accustomed to desire and seduction, but she did something to him that completely undid his brain and made him mad, made him want to do things that no gentleman should.

He wanted—bloody hell—he wanted to steal her away, pull her clothes from her, lay her back in the lavender fields, and worship her body until she cried out his name. His real name...

But none of that mattered.

No, because while she was helping him, whenever he came into a room, she said a few words of polite discourse, then exited. Whenever they were together, she stayed apart from him, and he could not blame her.

They were not here for intimacy. They were here to get a job done, and it was happening rather swiftly, much to his relief and no doubt hers.

Her aid was vital. She arranged information and meetings for him.

Bilby was appalling. The stable boys, Tom, George, and Michael, had let him know that they were paid wages, of course, but Bilby extracted wages for their upkeep. Usually, when one was a servant, one was given lodging and food for free. It was part of the wage. Bilby was extorting the boys.

It was disgusting.

Their families were poor, they needed every penny that they got, and Felix had a very strong idea where the money was going.

Little bits here and there. Bilby took and put them into his own pocket.

As they crossed over the land adjacent to Bodmin Moor, Felix could not stop looking at the beauty of the place. As appalling as Bilby was, this was a country so shockingly stunning, he hardly believed he was on Earth. He felt that he had to be in some mythic place.

He kept glancing over at Alice, too, but she was clearly determined not to have idle conversation with him.

"I'm sorry," he said at last, unwilling to endure this.

"I beg your pardon?" she called, as if she had not heard him.

"I'm sorry," he said again. "I did not mean to give you offense. I have the utmost respect for you, and I enjoy our conversation. You showed me a great deal of kindness and I…"

She whipped her gaze to him, and the look was so intense, he immediately stopped speaking. "We don't need to discuss it."

"Discuss…"

"*It*," she gritted.

"The kiss?" he queried, feeling at sea by how she made him feel.

"There was no kiss," she bit out.

"No," he said. "There wasn't. I wish there was now."

"Why?" she exclaimed.

"Because you are treating me as if I did kiss you," he pointed out. "I wish I had the pleasure for the pain."

She narrowed her eyes. "What a thing to say."

"I apologize, truly," he rushed, confused by his feelings. He'd never faced anything like this before. He knew that she desired him, too, but this was no simple affair. "Can we not go back to the banter that we had before? You are the only person that I find I can have genuine conversation with, and I don't have to lie about myself."

"You did that to yourself," she pointed out. "I have no sympathy for you."

He laughed at that. "I suppose I expect nothing less. You are an unyielding woman, and I like you better for it."

She blew out a harsh breath as she increased her stride over the rough ground. "Still, you are an earl. I tend flowers and make teas and perfumes in a small apothecary. You know where we live. Kissing me would be a terrible idea."

"It wouldn't be a terrible idea," he countered honestly. "It would only be a terrible idea if I misused you."

She narrowed her eyes. "Don't men like you always misuse people like me? Please. Understand. I must be very careful. I do not know you. And yet I allowed myself to be most… It is not you I am angry with. It is myself. People of your class throw away people of mine as if we are a bit of rubbish."

"That is not always true," he said, horrified by her words and yet understanding them. "But you have a point."

"Good." She nodded, her anger diminishing. "I'm glad that you know I do."

He scowled. She did. If ladies weren't careful, they could be ruined swiftly, and while desire was something that he thought perfectly normal and admirable, he could understand why she did not wish to trust him.

"But you did feel something," he ventured before he could stop himself.

"Why are you asking me this?" she demanded. "Is your sense of manhood so fragile?"

He laughed again. "With you? Certainly. You are a fiery, fascinating creature, and at every turn, I am amiss."

"No, you are not," she countered, throwing her hands up into the air.

"I am," he insisted. "You have to correct me all the time."

"That is only because you are learning," she said, turning to him. "It is clear to me that you are a master out there in the real world. It is only here on this estate where you do not know things."

He stayed his distance, since she was gifting him with conversation again, though he dearly longed to cross to her again. "Are you saying that if I got you into my world, things would be different?"

"I'll never be in your world," she said flatly. "There! There's the Perkins house."

He looked across to where she was pointing. It was a small cottage with a wind-twisted tree beside it.

"You can't be serious," he said, anger bubbling inside him, replacing any thought of Alice and lavender fields.

"Oh, I am."

"They pay rent?" he growled.

"Yes, they do."

"Why in God's name would they stay here like this?" he demanded, his gaze searching the hovel, as if he could find answers there.

"Mr. Perkins has lived there for years," she explained, her voice full of sorrow. "They lived here before you owned the estate. When you bought it, Mr. Perkins felt too old to leave. And of course, his wife died here and their children grew up here. The old man, he doesn't want to leave. It gives him memories, you see."

He ground his teeth. What was he doing speaking of kisses and desires when someone was living in utter misery on his land? He wanted to kick himself.

"I should have come sooner," he rasped, his disappointment in himself pounding in his head.

"I'm glad that you've come at all," she stated. "Others wouldn't have done so. They would've ignored any signs of difficulty and let it be run while they kept their peace and their coin."

"That is not what we should do," he ground out as his hands curled into fists. He was grateful Bilby wasn't within a mile. "That sort of cruel peace is not what life should be about."

Her eyes flared at his harsh declarations, as if he had startled her.

"You don't think keeping the peace is important?"

He snorted. "I suppose you're going to say that's privileged of me."

"It is," she said honestly. Her violet eyes were full of admiration now. "You're also right. I think if more of us shed that kind of peace, we'd have a better life."

"Is that what you're going to do when you go to London?" he asked. "Break the peace?"

She gave a tight nod. "My mother will be very disappointed. I am her dearest caretaker and her friend. It'll be very hard for her for me to leave."

"But you have to go," he urged.

She swallowed. The muscles of her throat worked as she did so. He could not tear his eyes away from the delicate skin of her throat, the way her body moved. She was captivating. He had known so many women, so many powerful, elegant women. Women with dowries, women who had trained themselves in how to enamor a man, and none of them had anything on Alice Wright.

At least, not with him.

"You must go to London, Alice," he said. "Peace is not worth staying."

"It is easy for you to say so," she countered as she stared at Mr. Perkins's cottage, hoping that this introduction was a wise decision. "You don't seem to have any connections."

He winced at that. "It is on purpose."

"Why would you do that to yourself?" she asked, her body tensing.

"Connection leads to pain."

"But—"

"That's enough, Alice. We each have our reasons for how we live."

The intensity of his reply cut through the air and she winced. "You're right. It's none of my business."

He nodded, hating that he had been so terse, but he had no wish to speak of his past. "You've made it very clear. We should keep our distance, so let's not share our deepest selves. There's no need."

Her face paled, but then she gave a tight nod and strode toward the house.

"Mr. Perkins, it's Alice Wright."

"Come in," a voice called from the other side of the splintered panel.

Felix noted the frailness of it. She pushed open the door and carried her basket in.

"I've brought some things for you," she said as she opened

the door and went in. "Mother sent you an ointment for your knee, and I've got bread and milk and cheese. And honey."

"How very kind of you, my girl," Mr. Perkins said from his chair by the small fire.

Felix followed Alice in and tried not to look appalled.

The ceiling was worse than a rat's warren. The thatch of it was coming undone. He could scarce believe his eyes. Stones in the walls were starting to come apart. There were chinks where plaster should have been put in.

"How'd you do, Mr. Perkins?" he said, offering his hand to the old man. "I'm Mr. Summers, the new man at the stable."

"Ah, I've heard about you, big strong man." Mr. Perkins offered a shaking, gnarled palm. They clasped hands, and then the old man smiled weakly, but his eyes shone with the pleasure of visitors. "Come, sit down. Come, sit down. I don't have anything strong to offer you to drink, but I do have tea. Just a bit of it. Or you could have hot water with honey."

"I'll take hot water with honey, Mr. Perkins, if that's all right with you."

"Wonderful," he said. "My dear Alice, would you be so kind? My hands have a mind of their own these days."

"Nothing would give me greater pleasure, Mr. Perkins," she said gently. Alice immediately went about the work, tidying the area that Felix supposed was meant to be the kitchen.

"Are you all alone here, Mr. Perkins?" he asked.

He nodded. "My children have gone off into Bodmin. They work there, you see. They don't want to be on the moors anymore, and I don't blame them. It's very difficult to farm here and the world is changing. I'm happy that they've gone and found jobs in shops. This estate just isn't what it was."

"I'm very sorry to hear it," he said, his heart aching for all that had clearly been lost. "Would you care to tell me about that?"

Mr. Perkins' face grew wary.

"I'm sorry," Felix assured. "I didn't mean to make you feel uncomfortable."

"That's all right." His face transformed as memories came to him. "My wife and I were very happy here. We moved here when we were a young couple, and we thrived. The house was wonderful, but I'm too old to fix it now, myself."

"And no one fixes it for you, Mr. Perkins?" Felix sat quietly, but his insides raged with a sense of injustice.

He shook his head. "No."

Felix frowned. "Surely, the rain comes in."

Mr. Perkins chuckled. "Oh, it does. It does. Every night is a very exciting state of affairs. I never know if I'm going to be rained on, snowed on, or have a good night. I can even see the stars sometimes, you know."

"That's not right, Mr. Perkins," he said flatly.

"Right or not, it is the way of it," Mr. Perkins replied.

"Not for long," he vowed, the words coming from deep within him.

"That Bilby, he's difficult. I don't think you'll change his mind, though good lad you are for saying you'll say something."

Felix was going to do more than say something. He knew that he had money allocated for the improvement and upkeep of the cottages on his lands. He'd even allocated funds to have new cottages built. Cottages that were strong and free of damp so his tenants could have good lives. Where the bloody hell was the money going? He had a fairly good enough idea, and now he knew what needed to be done.

He needed to get into Bilby's books.

"Bilby likes the big house," Perkins said.

"I beg your pardon?" he asked, astonished.

Perkins nodded as Alice handed him a mug of hot water with honey. "Spends a great deal of time there, that's what my friend tells me."

"He does, does he?" Felix leaned forward, trying to show how interested he was but give no alarm.

Perkins nodded his silver head and took a small sip before he sighed with pleasure. "Yes. There are rumors he even sleeps there," Mr. Perkins added, as if he was delivering the most delicious bit of gossip, and in truth, he was.

Felix caught Alice's eye as she poured out the rest of the hot water into mugs and stirred honey into them. She passed a drink to Felix and paused as their fingertips touched for a moment.

She licked her lips, then pulled away. Alice faced the brown bread, sawed it vigorously, and spread rich butter upon it.

"You are a font of information, Mr. Perkins," Felix said before waving his hand at Alice to make sure she did not serve him bread and butter.

He would take none of this man's stores. In fact, he needed to make certain the fellow got a good ham. He needed sustenance.

Mr. Perkins lifted his finger to his nose, as if to say he could keep a secret. "I shouldn't talk out of turn, but I like you. There's something about you that tells me you are very capable, as is Miss Alice. You two would make a fine pair now, wouldn't you?"

Alice snapped up straight. "Mr. Perkins, you know I have absolutely no intention of marrying."

"It's a waste," Mr. Perkins protested, warming his hands with his mug. "You're a fine woman, and you should have a fine man who knows how to make you happy. I think he could make you happy. You could make her happy, couldn't you, Mr. Summers?"

"I am certain that I do not have the capacity to meet all of her needs," Felix said carefully. He did not wish to spark her ire.

Mr. Perkins grinned. "Ha, you're only saying that so you won't irk her. I can see it in your eyes, my boy."

"What can you see?" he asked.

"You think the world of our Miss Alice, don't you? And it's only been a few days. Tells me you're a very intelligent fellow."

He was a fool, actually, because he did like Alice Wright a great deal, and she wanted nothing to do with him.

Chapter Ten

Felix strode to the edge of the village, trying to shake off the rage pumping through him.

The mill had not been replaced.

Was there anything Bilby had accomplished from the intersections for the estate that Felix had sent since the purchase of the estate? Had the man succeeded in anything? As far as Felix could tell, the only thing that Bilby had succeeded in was pocketing funds or letting everything fall to rack and ruin.

What was the man going to do if Felix suddenly showed up not as a horse trainer, but as the Earl of Enderley?

What in God's name could the man say? Was he suddenly going to fly into the night with all his profits? The thought actually resonated. Yes, that was likely exactly what Bilby was going to do.

If Bilby got word Felix was coming to the estate, he might very well fly into the night, performing a flit, taking his ill-gotten gains to somewhere like Australia or the New World.

The man was a cesspit, and Felix couldn't wait to get all

of the proof necessary, but he needed more accounts of what had happened.

He'd sent money for a new mill to be built on the river so that the locals could have their grain ground into flour and bread might be affordable for all. He'd even provided a yearly wage for a miller. But alas, it seemed that no such thing was in sight, as far as Felix could tell. The old mill on the river was standing idle at present and falling into disarray.

He strode further into the village, winding his way around chickens, pigs, dogs, children chasing hoops and balls, then headed toward the best source of information in town. Well, perhaps the second best. He was fairly certain the first resided with the women of the village doing laundry, but he doubted he would be able to insinuate himself easily into such company.

So he chose the tavern instead.

There were several gentlemen conversing outside near the trough meant for horses, smoking their pipes, having a chat.

Felix gave them a nod, then strode past them, pushed the heavy oak door open that looked like it had seen centuries of trade, and headed into the surprisingly bright room. It was late afternoon. Most of the men had finished their work and liked to come in for a chat, which he found to be generally a good thing for the morale of any group of people.

The getting together of individuals to vent their daily frustration was extremely healthy and vital to the well-being of all.

He headed up to the bar, placed his elbow on the long piece of wood, and waited to be served. He stopped and spotted a dog sitting just at his feet. The animal, a herding dog, plunked his bum on the ground. His short tail wagged swiftly, and his pink tongue lolled out of his mouth as he panted. A pair of bright blue eyes blinked up at Felix.

"Who's a good boy?" he said as he reached down and scratched the fellow behind his ear.

"He often doesn't like strangers, sir," an older man observed, his face creased with wrinkles from the toil of hard work and time. "But he seems to think that you are just fine. Are you the new man up at the estate?"

"I am that," he affirmed cordially.

Felix eyed what the man was drinking, standing at the bar. He did not usually come to such establishments. Occasionally, he went to the East End, but if he went to the East End, he drank gin. This did not seem to be an establishment that served gin, which was a good thing. Gin often brought people to very low places, especially if they were in a financially difficult state.

He eyed the amber liquid in the other man's frothing mug. "I'll have what he's having," he said to the barman, who was wiping a towel over the bar top.

The barman whipped the fabric over his big shoulder, then turned to pour out the beverage from the tap of a large barrel.

The man beside Felix had wiry gray hair, but he could not tell if the fellow was forty or sixty. There was something about the way that life must have taken the man down, and yet there was a spark in his eyes that suggested that nothing had defeated him.

"I like animals," Felix explained honestly. "They are often far more comforting than people."

"Ah, and this is why you work with the horses," the man said, then took a drink of his ale.

Felix smiled. "Indeed, it is."

And the truth was he did like animals. Not above people, but they were different. They provided a certain peace that humans never could, what with humans' ability to lie and to be unreliable. Animals were extremely reliable and very predictable, and so he reached down and scratched the dog again behind the ear.

"He's such a good fellow," he enthused.

"Indeed," the older man agreed, a look of pride transforming his face. "And he knows how to herd a group of sheep with the best of them."

The older man smiled down at his dog, but he did not pat him as he took another long drink of ale.

"May I ask your name, sir?" Felix asked, straightening.

"Davey Holden," the man said.

"Davey, it's a pleasure to meet you. I'm Summers."

The man gave him a nod. "Hello."

The crowd was beginning to gather into the dimly lit establishment, people coming around as the light began to fall. The fire in the hearth crackled, giving the place a warm glow, and the barmen went about lighting lanterns.

"It seems to be a lovely village," Felix observed, wishing to put the man at ease. "I'm looking forward to settling down here."

"It is that," Holden agreed. "We're all proud and pleased of it." But then there was a strange note to his voice.

"There seems to be something there that you wanted to say," Felix prompted, keeping his voice friendly and inviting.

Holden hesitated as if weighing his choices. "Well, you are new in town, and I wouldn't wish to give you any difficulty."

"Difficulty?" he echoed.

Holden cleared his throat. "At the estate."

And then he knew he had an in.

"Bilby," Felix mused. "Odd fellow that. I've only met him the once, and I'm not entirely certain what I thought. He's my employer. So of course I must be respectful."

"Forgive me," Holden cut in. "But he's not your employer. The earl is your employer. He owns Helexton, but Bilby acts on the earl's behalf." Holden frowned into his ale. "And sometimes I think if the earl knew what that man was up to…"

Holden hesitated before he let out a tired sigh.

"Yes?" Felix prompted, his curiosity growing, hoping the man would speak.

"Well, there are rumors about what Bilby does to the earl's books, but everyone knows that he extorts the village."

"I beg your pardon?" he said, his gut clenching as if he had been delivered a blow.

Holden locked gazes with him. "The earl owns the village, of course, and he could have all of us out in a moment. He could move the entire town, if he was displeased. And Bilby makes certain that wherever he goes, he doesn't have to pay for anything." Holden hesitated. "Since my dog likes you, I know you're a decent man. And so I feel compelled to warn you. You should be careful. He'll take advantage of you if he can. Any money you have? Don't keep it in your lodging. Find a secure place for it. Bury it if you have to. Bilby's notorious for finding reasons to filch people. All over the village, he does it."

"My God," Felix said, resisting the urge to grit his teeth. "Is this true?"

The land agent wasn't just cheating Felix… He was cheating people who could ill afford it. Rage stoked in his belly at the injustice of it.

"It is," the man warned. "So you be careful, lad."

He was struck by Holden's kindness in looking out for him.

"There's a mill out on the river, but it seems out of use," Felix began, hoping for clarification. "Is there not a miller who takes care of the flour?"

Holden let out a dry laugh. "Oh, yes. It's Bilby's man. Charges terrible prices for flour, he does. He had it improved not long ago. It's further down the river, off of the estate."

"In truth?" he prompted.

Holden nodded before he finished off his ale.

Felix stared at his own tankard, the bitterness in his gut so intense, he had no wish to drink. "And do you have proof that Bilby is doing these things?"

Half the men in the bar turned to him at his shocked question, and they all began to laugh.

"Proof, Summers?" Holden asked. "What do you mean proof?"

"Something in writing?" he clarified.

A big man across the room turned to them and rumbled, "We don't need writing. He's done it to most of the men in town. He's done it to most of the men in this *room*. We'll all happily vouch for it. But we have to be careful, and you have to be careful, too, because if Bilby gets wind of us doing anything against him, he'll evict us all, you see? And then where will we be? Most of our families have lived on our farms for hundreds of years."

"Hear, hear," another man said, lifting his tankard. "I can't leave my cottage. My great-great-grandparents built that place. It's been our family blood for well over a hundred years, and we're not about to leave that land. But Bilby? He could force us off of it, and then where would we go and what would we have?"

Felix nodded, the gravity of the situation sinking in. "I see. And the Earl of Enderley, has anyone thought of writing to him?"

"No," a young, wiry man tsked. "Why would we do that? He's far away in London. Never came here. Shows no interest in us whatsoever. Surely, he has no desire to champion a bunch of village people. He's never even come to meet us."

That hit hard. It was true. He had never come to meet them, and now he felt a failure in this. He should have come a long time ago.

He should have assured them that he would be their man and that he would do all he could to improve their lot in life. It was, after all, what a good landowner was supposed to do. In that moment, he realized he was a terrible landowner. He left all of his estates to the care of others, not just this one, so that he could focus on his work at Horse Guards.

And that was going to change today.

As soon as he could, he was going to send letters off to his solicitors, stating that he would visit every single one of his estates this year, to make certain that things were in good order and that the people on his lands knew they could always count on him.

But the war...

He swallowed. It had taken up so much of his time, so much of his thoughts And he did not have time to waste. London needed him. The war effort needed him. Napoleon would wait for no man.

"Do you think we could perhaps make sure that Bilby lost his job?" Felix blurted.

Holden shook his head doubtfully. "He's a very powerful man with a lot of money around here."

He nodded, realizing he couldn't push more without giving away too much. "Thank you for the warning. I'll take it."

And with that, he drank several sips from his tankard, took coin from his pocket, left it on the bar, then headed out to the door.

He didn't want to keep them in a sour mood.

After all, talking about Bilby seemed to displease the entire room, and he thought it rather noble of them all to warn him. And he was pleased at the information he'd received.

Extortion of the village? Threats of eviction? Bilby was worse than he ever could have imagined, and no one had told him because he'd been so distant.

He headed out onto the road.

"There you are," a voice called.

He whipped toward it. All at once, he felt... Bloody hell. What he felt... It was a mixture of tension and hunger at once. Hunger for her. And tension because he could never have her.

He blew it out, determined to seem at ease.

Alice folded her arms over her chest. "Drinking, are you? Becoming a man of the village?"

Her eyes were twinkling with merriment.

"Oh indeed, indeed, Miss Alice," he said, tugging at his forelock, and then with a grin, for he couldn't deny that the very sight of her filled him with pleasure. Without delay, he headed toward her. "I've gotten some very interesting information. Has Bilby ever tried to extort your mother?"

Her eyebrows raised. "I beg your pardon?"

"Threatened to have you kicked off of your apothecary if you don't—"

"No, he has not," she rushed, her eyes skittering about as if making sure no one could hear them, "and I think it's because we rent so much land on the estate." She drew in a frustrated breath. "But if that's what you found out, I'm glad you did. And it seems to me as if all of the work that we've been doing is paying off?"

"It will." He nodded, the muscle at his jaw tightening with his resolve.

She eyed him up and down. "They didn't suspect a single thing?"

He shook his head. "They did not. Thank you for the outfit and also the readjustment in thinking."

"That's all that I did," she said cheerfully. "Nothing more. You took my advice, and you now seem to be doing what needs to be done with skill. You'll not give yourself away in the pursuit of Bilby's downfall. Will you be able to do it?"

"Never you fear on that score. As soon as I have it in

writing, I'm taking that man down. And of course, now I have several accounts from the villagers, and once they know that the earl is on their side, they won't be afraid to testify."

She gazed upon him then with admiration.

And that look, that single look of approval, caused his world to spin.

Chapter Eleven

Felix could not sleep.

He had not slept well since Alice had entered into his life, a short week ago, and it was worse knowing that she was but a few feet from him.

He was lucky to have a small room to himself. Something he had realized, living in the cramped but loving quarters. But it was his due as a lodger, who paid his way. And Mrs. Wright and the family seemed quite pleased to have the extra coin that afforded them better meat, or so he had overheard the other morning.

Mrs. Wright had been delighted as she'd prepared the day's stew, all but crowing over the good cuts.

His stomach had twisted, knowing that even with their shop, they struggled. And yet they did not struggle in affection for each other.

And then there was Alice... The way she moved, the way her fiery eyes lit when in conversation, the way her hair teased across her face... How he wished he could kiss her neck the way the locks of her hair did.

The shop was small, the rooms close together, and as he laid on his bed slightly too small for his frame, in his room, staring up at the ceiling, he let out an exhale of frustration.

He turned over, bending his legs so that he just fit. It was one of the curses of being tall. Usually, he did not mind. But he was already struggling to fall off into the land of Orpheus.

Alice had lit him aflame.

Bloody hell, there was no denying it. He was well and truly gone. Not only did he desire her, he admired her. She was a fascinating creature, consuming him. Desire had stolen half his wits.

Felix threw himself on his back again and stared up at the simple ceiling, threw an arm over his head, and let out an exhale. What was he going to do? How was he going to make it through all of this?

He did not know. Perhaps he should simply turn tail for London and fire Bilby without any more to do here in Cornwall. The ruse was still simple…save for how his damned body kept responding to Alice Wright.

But she had proved invaluable. The information from Mr. Perkins, the way she had led him over the estates, it was singular.

She was unique. In every way.

Damnation. With thoughts of her lacing through his brain, sleep would never come.

So he threw his legs over the side of the bed and planted his feet on the floor. Felix thrust a hand through his hair, unable to stay still a moment longer. His body was all but pumping with need for her. How he longed to taste her lips, to skim his lips along her throat, to tease her clavicles, then pull her gown down and trace the perfect curves of her breasts with his tongue.

Damnation. That would only be the beginning. How he longed to rake his hands along the curve of her ribs, stroke her waist, divest her of her garments, and then after causing her cheeks to crest pink with pleasure, he would thrust deep into her welcoming heat.

It was a mad fantasy. But it was one he could not seem to shake from his mind.

No, just as he couldn't shake her scent, or the way her hair teased her chin, or the way she bandied words with him without any sort of deference.

Felix curled his hands into fists, dug his nails into his palms, then stood.

There was really only one thing for it, given the circumstance.

Fresh air.

He pulled his clothes on quickly and decided a walk was the only thing that would drive this feeling from him. Surely if he walked, he would be able to go to sleep. It did not matter that he had worked all day. He had mucked out the stables with the boys. He had taken care of all of the tack. He had ridden every single horse. None of it had driven her from his system.

It did not matter that this was the hardest he had physically worked in years and the new blisters on his hands would soon be calluses. He was in fine condition. He spent a great deal of time at Gentlemen Jackson's, and every day he practiced the art of dueling.

It was important for a man of his status to keep up his abilities with a rapier and pistol.

Still, this had been different. It was a different sort of physical labor. He'd savored the ache in unfamiliar muscles. And yet he could not close his eyes and make his mind stop wandering to her, to her bright eyes, her bright mind…her mouth that promised bliss…

This was the bloody devil. His mind was at it again. In a moment, he'd imagine her beneath him as he rocked his cock into her core, bringing her to ecstasy as he stroked her—

Felix mouthed a curse and pulled his boots on, crossed to the door, and then very carefully crept out into the hall. He did not want to creak over the floorboards, and given the age of the place, it would be an easy thing to do.

It was the sort of house one might have expected out of a storybook, a nursery rhyme. There were dark wood beams everywhere, wattle and daub, and nooks and crannies.

The stairs were ancient, and he slipped down, hoping that he would not awaken the house. But as he was heading out, he realized he was not the only person awake this night. There were sounds coming from one of the back rooms.

He paused, curiosity piqued. Curiosity had long been a part of his nature and another thing he could not ignore. Felix slowly turned away from the front door and crept through the shadowy house.

He paused in the open doorway of the kitchens.

Moonlight spilled through the windows, a fire crackled in the hearth, and *she* stood there working by candlelight. Her body was silhouetted before the fire, leaving her in a sort of heavenly glow.

She arched, reaching upward, which caused her breasts to press against the bodice of her gown as she pulled herbs down that were hanging from the ceiling.

Slowly, her fingers working as if bewitched by magic, plucked the petals from their stems, dropped them into a mortar and pestle, and began grinding away.

Her shoulders bowed, her head tilted, and her arm worked as she gripped that stone pestle, using it skillfully. The way she held that pestle in her hand brought other things to mind...his body...

Could she hold him with such a firm grip, transfixed?

He swallowed and tried to shake the image from his mind.

After all, she was a sight to behold as she did the thing that she loved so well. She was completely focused on her task. Her body moved easily as she leaned against the table. He took a step back, not wishing to invade her privacy, and then of course he stepped on a floorboard, which creaked.

She flinched and whirled around to face him. "Oh, goodness," she exclaimed. "I thought it was one of the children and I'd have to put them back up to bed."

"I am not an errant child," he teased, wondering how she ever felt at peace, knowing that she might be interrupted at any moment by her boisterous but delightful siblings. The only experience he'd had of such things had been here, in this house. He'd grown up alone, surrounded by caretakers.

And the truth was he felt like an errant schoolboy at this moment, catching sight of the object of his desires. If he wasn't thirty and a rake, he might have blushed, caught thinking the things he was thinking about her hand and his...

"May I?" he asked, gesturing to the room.

"Of course," she said.

Clearing his throat, he crossed in slowly.

Her blond hair was silvery in the moonlight, her skin golden from the flames. A mixture of all that was precious, and then there were the things of the earth. The scents wafting toward him were heady. He wasn't certain what caused them. All he knew was they awakened his mind, just as she did.

"Whatever are you doing?" he queried.

"Preparing some remedies," she said.

He frowned, surprised. "You're not making perfumes?"

"No. Alas," she sighed with a playful smile. "I do not have nearly as much time for that as I would like, and most of that work is done up at the big house."

"Truly?" he asked, stunned by how little she could attend to her dreams.

His entire life was framed around his wants and needs.

"Indeed," she replied. "But I do as much as I can. We must make money, you see, and my mother makes most of the money to raise us from providing things for the villagers and other locals here to ensure that they are well."

"'Tis a noble endeavor," he said, his body warming with his admiration for her.

She nodded, then her nose wrinkled with distaste. "Not everyone is so grateful, though. Sometimes people can be…"

"Yes?" he prompted, his curiosity about her life piquing.

She looked away from him and studied the table and its contents. "Well, sometimes people need someone to blame when things don't go as they hope."

He took another step toward her, wishing he could remove the discomforts from her life. "I understand that," he said before he ventured, "Are people ever unkind?"

She hesitated. "There have been a few times, yes, and even once or twice when people have accused my mother of being in league with the devil."

"Your mother?" he exclaimed loudly.

Her brows flared at his volume.

And he now deliberately whispered, "Are people mad in this town?"

A rueful laugh slipped past her delicious lips. "I know it sounds absurd if you're a person of reason, and in the times of Rousseau and Voltaire, but alas, many country people still believe in the old ways. They believe that fairies inhabit trees and that women can summon the devil and dance with him by the fire."

"I should like to have discourse with someone who believes that," he said, longing to seize any such idiot and teach them or thing or two with his fists.

"No, you would not," she warned with an arched brow.

He groaned. "You're right. I would not, and I'm sorry to make light of it. It must be very terrible for you."

She shrugged. "It is part of life. Surely, difficult things happen for you?"

He nodded, his stomach clenching. "Sometimes I have to tell families that their sons, husbands, fathers aren't coming home. It happens far more often than I'd like, if I'm honest. I lose people that I have trained... And they don't die easy deaths. I can't protect them when..."

He swallowed the rest of his words, shocked that he had nearly spoken of far more than he should.

"I'm so sorry," she said softly.

"Thank you." He drew in a breath. "We all have the difficulties that we must bear."

"In all honesty, yours sound far more difficult than mine."

"They're not," he countered as he sucked in a breath. "Not really." He moved closer to her then, wishing to end this sad line of discourse, and looked down at the pestle. "What will you do with this?"

She blinked, her breaths increasing. "I will steep it and then mix it to create a tincture."

"A tincture," he said, shaking his head.

"Yes, that can be taken orally," she explained.

"And what will it do?"

"This one will help calm the nervous system," she explained. "Many people are so overworked and so afraid about the war and various changes that are happening, they need this. It soothes them, you see."

He lowered his head ever so slightly and whispered, "Do you feel anxious about the war and change?"

"I am hopeful that we shall see great things from all that is evolving around us," she said, squaring her shoulders as if she refused to be cowed by the tide of life. "I have to choose hope or I would never leave the house or my bed."

"Ah, and you accused me of being silly for optimism," he teased, drawn in by her, drawn in by his awe of her. "You are just the same."

She laughed at that. "I suppose I am. By the way," she said gently, "the way you were with Mr. Perkins? I admired it very much. Thank you for being so kind to him."

"You don't have to thank me, Alice," he said. "He's a good man, and he's been treated terribly. I'll soon right it."

She nodded, then returned to her work, taking the crushed herbs, putting them into oil.

He dared to rest his hand upon the table next to hers, but a breadth away. It felt like a shocking thing to do, and yet he could not stop himself. "Will you teach me what you are doing?"

Stilling, she let her hand linger next to his. "You wish to be taught how to make a tincture?"

"Why ever not?" he asked, his voice a low rumble to his own ears.

"All right," she said. "Come."

She let her hand slide from the table, studied the dried herbs and flowers hanging from the ceiling, and began to reach. She went up on tiptoe, her body a beautiful arc, but the flowers were just out of reach.

Felix did not think, only crossed behind her and raised his arm to gently grasp it for her. As he did so, his chest brushed her shoulders, and her hips teased against him.

She hesitated, her eyes fluttering closed, but then she stepped away.

He said nothing because he had done nothing that was truly out of propriety, but the shocks of need that traveled through him—and he was certain, her—were startling.

Wordlessly, he handed her the bunch of flowers.

"What is this?" he asked.

"Chamomile." She stroked the dried petals.

He swallowed as he watched her fingers skim over the flowers, and he wondered what it would be like to have her hands skim over his limbs.

"Ah. Such an interesting name, such a little flower."

"It is a powerful flower," she emphasized. "It helps some people sleep, and it calms others."

"And this?" he asked, pointing to a different flower on the table.

"St. John's Wort," she informed in a factual tone. "We are going to make a tea."

"I see," he said.

"Now." She cleared her throat, placed the flowers on the table, and then smoothed her hands down the front of her gown. "Help me pluck the flowers off."

Felix followed her instruction, doing so slowly, one by one.

They worked in companionable silence until they had filled up the mortar. She took the pestle in her hand firmly. "Now come here," she said. "Put your hand over mine."

Again, he followed her instruction, gently placing his hand over hers.

His hand all but swallowed hers up, and he could not draw his gaze away from the sight.

She licked her lips and whispered, "Good. Now I want you to feel the rhythm of it."

And then she began to rock the pestle around the bowl. He was paying attention, but he could not stop the overwhelming sensation of being near to her, the scent of her hair, the feel of her closeness.

It was heady.

Slowly, she turned to face him and tilted her head back. "This is a coil," she said.

"In what way? Am I making a mistake?"

"No," she breathed. "I want to kiss you, and you want to kiss me, but we mustn't."

"Why not?" he rumbled softly, his breath quickening. The

air changed about them as it grew thick with the possibility of passion.

"You know very well why not," she protested fiercely but quietly. Her eyes searched over his face, perplexed. "I have dreams."

"I'm not going to stand in the way of your dreams, Alice," he assured, even as his body heated with her nearness, at her admission. "I'm going to help you reach them."

"But this thing between us," she rasped, gesturing with her hand back and forth between their bodies. "What if—" She swallowed and shook her head, looking away.

"I see you're afraid," he said gently.

"Do you really see?" she mocked slightly.

"Indeed, I do, Alice." He drew in a breath, uncertain if he should speak what he saw, but...he did not wish her to think him frivolous or uncaring. "You're afraid that your life will be like your mother's, that you will become trapped behind a counter and that you will never be able to do the things that you wished. But I have no desire to trap you behind a counter, Alice. I do not wish to marry you or have many children with you. I don't want that life for you. You're not the sort of woman I would marry."

"Right," she said, her gaze snapping to his. Her mouth pressed into a line before she bit out, "Of course. I am far beneath you."

"No," he cut in quickly, wishing he could kick himself for his ill-thought-out reply. "That is not it."

"Why, then?"

It was his turn to look away. He'd never before dared to say what he was about to. "Because," he began, "you're the sort of woman that I would come to care about deeply if I was not careful, and I want to tell you right now, I will not allow myself to fall in love with you and marry you, Alice. Not for anything. Not for the world."

"Oh," she said softly. "What has made you thus?"

He would not allow himself to think of the tear-stained letters he had read from loved ones left behind. The agony of relaying the news of the deaths of loved ones and seeing the pain of those left behind.

It was something he wanted no part of and certainly did not wish to inflict on someone else.

"I have very strict rules for myself," he said honestly. "Just as you seem to have very strict rules for yourself. I promised myself a long time ago that I would never, ever make a widow of a woman."

"You work in Horse Guard," she said. "Though essential, that is not the battlefield—"

"Yes," he agreed. "But things can happen, Alice. Accidents happen."

He thought of his dear friend, the Duke of Tynemore, whose wife had died in a tragic accident months ago.

The man seemed well to the world, but he was a shell of a man who could barely climb out of his misery. His insides were a sea of torture.

He weighed his words carefully. "I could not bear to love someone and leave them behind. It is the worst of all possible things. I've never been close to anyone," he explained. "I am selfish for others and myself, too. My parents died when I was young, and I do not wish to risk the cruelty of such a connection when I've never had one."

She softened at this. "My mother loved my father. That's why she married him and why she gave up her dreams, but there has always been a hollow ache to her. She doesn't regret having any of us, but she does regret the loss of the life she wanted so dearly." She blinked as if coming up from a reverie. "Will you *never* marry, then?"

He let out a rueful note. "Oh, I will have to marry one day," he said. "And when I do, when I ask the woman to marry me, it will be very clear what I want her for."

She flinched. "Oh, dear. A broodmare?"

He winced at that. "I wouldn't use that term exactly, but just given the nature of the aristocracy, it would be necessary that she provide me with an heir, and she will run my estates, and we will have a relationship that hinges on a mutual understanding of business. After all, marriage is just a contract, Alice."

Her jaw dropped. "For your kind of people, I suppose. How very cold," she surmised.

"How very *necessary*," he corrected. "And are you so very different, wanting to make sure that love does not get in the way of your dreams?"

She pursed her lips as she considered this. "I suppose we are the same."

"Then there is no reason why we cannot give in to our desire for each other."

"But...what about children?"

He tilted his head, surprised. He should not have been. So many ladies knew nothing of the making of children. And certainly nothing in the planning of having them or not.

Still, given the family business, he would have thought differently.

"Does your mother have nothing to say about the careful ways women can ensure that pregnancy is not required from intimacy?"

Her brow furrowed. "Have you seen how many children my mother has?"

He nodded. "Well, I promise you, there are ways we can be careful if you wish to indulge in the pleasures that can occur between us. This I promise, I will not allow any harm to come to you."

She gazed up at him. "I have never ever wanted anything like this before," she admitted. "If I'm honest."

"Nor have I," he breathed as the truth hit him hard. He had no idea what to do with that truth, but he couldn't examine it. No, thoughts were far too dangerous. Passion made more sense.

Captivated by her closeness, Felix wrapped his arms about her. He spread his palms along her back, and then he pulled her upward so that he might seize her mouth in a kiss. His lips played over hers. She tensed for a moment, but then she melted against him, her soft form fitting perfectly against his hard one.

He teased his tongue against her, and she opened to him. He could not hold back and delved into her welcome heat. A soft moan escaped her throat as she kissed him back, passionately.

Their tongues danced together, tentatively at first, then with a growing boldness and need. He slid his hand up her body and wove it into her hair. Each kiss was an intoxicating moment, pushing them, pulling them further into passion. He picked her up and placed her on the table.

He wanted to take her here, now. Shove all the flowers aside, lay her back, and feast on her body. But that would not do; he had to take his time. He had to give himself over only to the moment.

Felix gripped her hips and stepped between her legs. He did not want this to ever end. His blood was pumping wildly. His skin felt alive. He wanted to rip the clothes from their bodies and feel her pressed up against him, skin to skin.

It was an intense hunger that he had never experienced before, and he had no idea how to ignore it. He felt possessed almost, and as the kiss mounted, she tilted her head back, like an offering.

Slowly, he kissed along her throat, pausing at the hollow, captivated by that spot and the gentle scent of earth, Cornwall, the sea, and a collection of flowers he could not name.

Oh, how he wanted to make love to her. He massaged her hips, memorizing the feel of her, and just as he was about take a handful of her gown, he realized exactly what he was doing… He was about to ruin a young woman, staying in her house, and he could now recall the anger she'd felt at herself when they had almost kissed.

He couldn't be a cad. He couldn't be one of those men. As she had feared he might be.

Felix jolted back as if cold water had been sluiced over him.

Chapter Twelve

What was she doing?

This was so completely opposed to everything that Alice had promised herself—and yet it *felt* perfect. It was heaven, and suddenly she realized that all those promises could be kept and formed into new ones.

She wanted to experience exciting things. How could she create perfumes that mimicked passion when she knew so little of it herself? She pulled back from him, heady, enthralled, completely alive. "I did not know," she said.

He gazed down at her with hot eyes. "Nor did I," he said. He lifted a hand and stroked a lock of hair back behind her cheek.

"Do not tell me lies, my lord," she said with a rueful smile.

"My lord? Oh, Alice, you must call me Felix. How could you call me anything else after this? And it is not a lie," he murmured, cupping her chin and turning her face upward. "You are a wonder."

Felix… She was to call an earl by his given name. It felt momentous and dreamlike. Was she living a dream? She feared it might become a nightmare if she was not careful. But for now? For now, she would try to revel in all the good, all the wonder of it.

She slipped away from him. "But you're going to leave," she pointed out, her stomach tightening with the feeling of loss.

"Yes, and you are going to come with me," he countered.

She swallowed. "That's true."

"So I don't see why we cannot be the best of friends."

"Friends?" she echoed, the feelings swirling about her far from friendship, surely.

"Well," he said, considering this. "Friends and lovers. Is it not the very best of all things?"

She grinned at that, as she realized he was right. "Perhaps it is," she said brightly. "I could never imagine doing such a thing before."

"You're going to do so many things you never imagined," he said.

A floorboard creaked overhead, and they all but leaped back from each other.

She smoothed her hand over her curls as he adjusted his waistcoat.

"You must rise early, mustn't you?" she asked, searching for conversation.

He blew out a breath. "Indeed."

Her lips curved into a slow smile. "I've taught you how to make a tincture. Now I want you to teach me something."

"Teach you shat?" he queried, his eyes still burning with hunger for her, sparking with what he clearly wished he could do with her.

"Something fun," she blurted, her own body eager to give in, though her brain would not let her! She couldn't. Could she?

"Fun?" he echoed.

"Yes." She licked her lips and smoothed her hands down

the front of her gown to gather herself. "You said I'm going to do things I've never imagined before."

"Well," he began, "a vast array of opportunities awaits us."

She drew in a shaky breath. "Show me what life is full of. What adventures await."

He took her hand in his and lifted it to his lips. Slowly, as if he wished to memorize the feel of her, the taste of her, he kissed her palm. "It shall give me the greatest of pleasure, Alice."

"Tomorrow, then?"

"Tomorrow," he said.

• • •

Alice headed toward the stable-yard, wondering what the day would bring. The earl—*Felix*—had left very early, even before the sun was up. She wondered if he had slept at all, and she was a mix of various emotions. The whole evening had been quite an awakening, and now she did not know which way was up and which was down.

Thoughts racing through her head and anticipation humming through her veins, Alice crossed into the stable-yard.

The scent of hay, mud, and horse flesh filled the air. The laughter of the boys also filled the air, which gave her pause. She could not recall ever hearing so much laughter, but Felix was changing things. He was changing the recently grim culture at Helexton, and she was glad. Before Bilby had arrived, this place had been a very happy one, but recently it had fallen into disarray.

It was good to know it would return to a place of hope and good things.

"Ah, there she is," Felix called out, his booming voice rippling toward her. "Our lady fair!"

The boys cheered.

"How do you do, my lady?" Tom called.

"Very well, Sir Knight," she said back, with a quick curtsy. George and Michael ran forward and gave her flowers. Wild daisies that were a cheerful way to start the morning.

"Come. Come," they said. "You may be a lady, but today you are to be a warrior."

"I beg your pardon? I am not a lady," she pointed out, even as she allowed herself to be led forward. "I am a simple herbalist."

"There is nothing simple about you," Felix countered as he strode forward.

And much to her shock, she realized he was holding a long rapier. "Where the blazes did you get that?"

"The armory," he stated.

"The armory?" she yelped.

"Yes. It's a practice blade. Don't worry. I have permission from the housekeeper."

She gave him an appreciative look. The earl was the sort of man who knew how to make things happen. "You met the housekeeper, did you?"

"Yes. A very kind woman who seems strained under Bilby's hand. Luckily, I was able to convince her to be helpful," he said. "And I have promised her a box of chocolates from town for it. I think all is going to be well with her once I rid her of that man."

There it was again, Felix preparing to set all right with the world. And she truly believed he would, and she couldn't wait to see it.

"I'm glad to hear it," she said. "I feel quite sorry for her having to attend to Bilby all the time. Mrs. Brooke has always been kind to me. She brings me tea and cake when I'm working in the house."

She cleared her throat and pointed to the dulled rapier.

"But what are we going to do with that?"

He cocked his head to the side and contemplated the weapon. "You said you wish to learn something new."

Her eyes flared. "I didn't say I wanted to learn sword fighting."

"My lady fair!" cried George. "Do not be boring. I'd like to learn how to fight as well. If you will not, I volunteer!"

Tom laughed. "And me! And me!"

"Perhaps after," Felix said agreeably. "I shall teach the lady here first. Now you three go run about and do your work."

"All right," Michael said with a sigh. "But you have to promise you'll teach us when we come back."

"Of course," Felix assured. "If you do a good job's labor today, we shall have time to relax, and I shall happily teach you."

The three boys ran off, eager then.

Felix strode across the yard toward her, his linen shirt billowing about his hard form in the breeze. He held the rapier easily in his hand, outstretched, as if it was an extension of his name.

"*Why* this?" she asked, wary.

He tsked playfully. "Why? Why? Why? You did not want to get on the horse, but you enjoyed it, and I think you shall have a great fun with this as well."

"What if I turn you into a pincushion?" Her nerves prickled at the very idea. Accidentally killing an earl seemed a rather serious thing to do!

He laughed, then winked at her, a devilishly tempting thing. "I promise you I have been a pincushion before."

She gasped. "In truth?"

"Oh yes," he said. "I am not entirely made for indoor spaces."

She groaned, unable to tear her gaze away from his body,

which clearly knew physical pursuits. "You don't *look* as if you are made for indoor spaces," she said ruefully.

A slow, hot look filled his gaze, and suddenly she knew he was thinking of specific indoor pursuits that were vigorous and done best with her.

Heat coiled in her belly, and she couldn't quite breathe.

"I've spent a great deal of time dueling," he said, as if his mind was not on being alone with her. "And when one practices, sometimes one gets wounded."

"I would imagine," she said, trying to force her own mind to behave.

"Now, come here," he said, in that gravelly growl of his.

She did as he bid, thrilled with the idea of being able to do something so exciting.

"This is like a novel," she said.

"You do love to read," he agreed. "I thought you might enjoy learning something so adventurous as takes place in the books you admire."

"You are getting to know me too well, sir."

"I don't think I could ever know you *too* well, Alice," he said sincerely. "For the more I get to know you, the happier I feel."

She stared at him, stunned. Such things were dangerous things to say, but she felt the same, now that she had gotten over the fact that she had to stay away from him and she'd *had* to stay away from him because she liked him too well. Now, she didn't have to do that at all, and she had every intention of embracing it.

"Come here," he urged again. "Let me teach you how to hold it."

Her cheeks flushed. She did not know why, but as she stood before him, everything felt charged with the feelings between them.

"Now let me help you." He tucked her in front of him.

His hand slid to hers, and then he said, "Relax your grip. Relax it. You don't want to be tense."

She tried to do as he bid.

"Now, think of flowers," he urged, his eyes dancing with anticipation.

"Why flowers?"

He traced his fingers over hers. "You look very relaxed when you were working last night."

She could scarce keep her mind on his body, given his touch. "Oh."

"It's the same, really," he continued, his voice a hypnotic hum. "To be good at anything, you mustn't tense yourself. You must feel at ease."

"I have been working with flowers since I was born," she pointed out.

"And I have been holding a rapier since I was five," he said. "So I understand. Now..." He placed the hilt into her palm. She grasped it carefully, then gently clasped her fingers about it.

"Good," he said. "Very good. Now lift it."

"It's extremely heavy," she said, shocked at how it strained her arm.

He beamed at her. "Yes, it is. You'll develop quite good muscles if you take up sword-fighting."

She giggled, her own delight lightening the effort. "Imagine a lady sword-fighter."

"Stranger things have happened, Alice. The world is full of people who paved brave new roads."

What a thrilling thought that was! And she could not keep the way it thrilled her from forming a smile on her lips. "Now what?"

"Right," he said. "The first thing I'm going to teach you is how to thrust."

Her cheeks heated. "Shouldn't I learn to defend myself?"

"Oh, some people would say so, but I think that one should learn how to be on the offensive in this life. To go boldly," he said. "And then of course I will teach you how to defend. Now, what you will do..." He stood behind her, his chest to her back, and he eased down into a low straddle. "Mirror this," he instructed, and she did.

"Oh goodness," she murmured. "That is a very strange stance."

But what made it most strange was the way his body braced hers, skimming her back, her bottom, her thighs. And she could feel the ridges and valleys of his form.

It nearly stole all her rational thought.

And then he began to rock back and forth, back and forth.

"Follow my lead," he said, and again, without thinking, she did.

"Follow my breathing," he urged, and she allowed herself to breathe in slowly through her nose and then exhale.

As they began to breathe and move in unison, an inexplicable wave of wonder washed over her. She'd never felt so at ease or so capable before.

"Now, we're going to rock back, and then we're going to take a very strong step forward and thrust your arm forward at the same time."

He still had his hand about hers, guiding it gently.

Then as one, he pulled her back and then thrust forward.

She let out a note of surprise and felt herself go uneven. She tilted right, then tumbled back.

He clasped her carefully but beamed down at her. "Marvelous," he said. "Let's do it again."

Over and over, they repeated the action.

She felt herself getting flushed with the excitement of it all and the surprising amount of energy it took. They performed the task, again and again and again, until at last, she felt strong and confident.

"That's it," he praised. "Now do it yourself."

Felix stepped away from her, leaving her on her own. Shockingly, she felt bereft at the absence of his warm presence, but then she did exactly what he had done with her behind him. By herself.

A crow of triumph burst past her lips, and exhilaration raced through her.

"Well done," he said, applauding with those strong, beautiful hands of his.

"Now what?" she said, excited to continue working with him.

"I think we shall save the next lesson for tomorrow."

She resigned herself to it and handed him the practice blade. And surely, he wished to roust Bilby soon. "When will you come to the house to try to see the accounts?"

His face grew serious. "When are you planning to go up to the house next?"

"I can go now," she said. "Later this afternoon."

"Then let's do it," he said firmly. "The sooner we can wrench this place away from his control, and I can have him permanently barred from being a land agent, the better."

"The boys are very happy," she observed, touched by how Felix had changed their lives so swiftly.

He smiled. "They are, aren't they?"

"You're good at this," she informed.

"Good at what?" he asked, his brow furrowing.

"Making people happy," she said, her heart lifting. For it was true. Wherever he went, happiness seemed to follow. She did not know how she had gotten so lucky to have him in her life, providing the promise of good fortune, but she was still wary.

For in her experience, luck did not last, and so she would have to cling to this for as long as she could.

Chapter Thirteen

Alice loved Helexton despite the fact that Bilby had made it a misery in the years since he had taken over as land agent.

The house was heaven. It was one of the most beautifully made buildings she'd seen in her entire life. She had not traveled far from Cornwall, though.

As a matter of fact, she'd barely gone to Devon.

This house with its buttery yellow walls, the airy space inside, filled her with joy. On the dark days, it felt as if she had been transported into a blissful place. The beauty inside was almost impossible to take in. Frescoes were everywhere, beautiful white plasterwork depicting scenes from Ancient Greece.

Often, when she could, she stood staring at them for long hours, trying to imagine what it would've been like to have been in those ancient times, standing on Grecian hills, looking upon such heroes as Achilles and Odysseus.

She did not know if she would have loved being in Ancient Greece, but standing in Helexton, looking at the beautiful depictions of those people, she longed to know the olive trees and the various plants and flowers that came from a region that inspired such epic tales.

Surely, there would be beautiful flowers. Surely, there would be the most delicious of scents, scents she could turn into the most wonderful of perfumes. She would probably never go to Greece, so the frescoes would have to do instead.

Today, she walked past them quickly. She knew them well by memory in all events and headed to the herb room where they kept dry stores. She crossed in and smiled. It was four times the size of the kitchen in her mother's shop. It stretched on and on.

It was cool but not damp. Racks and rows of flowers and herbs hung from the ceiling, tied carefully upside down with her own hands over the last year. She worked tirelessly all of the time, making the lavender water, the rose water, the various perfumes and scents that would be used in the house.

Once upon a time, when the previous owners had lived here, there had been balls all of the time, and she had made tinctures and extractions for the cook to make rose puddings and lavender confections, but those days had long passed.

She wondered if the triumph would ever return to Helexton, where it was filled with laughter and beauty again. Perhaps it would, because after all, Felix was returning laughter outside of the great house. If he would but live inside, perhaps laughter could come back to this part of Cornwall, too, and others could enjoy and celebrate it.

She began to work, taking down flowers, bringing out jars, and considering which steps she needed to take next. She put on an apron and quickly set to completing her tasks.

She smiled to herself. Soon *he* would join her. Felix would come up from the stables and she would then find a way to whisk them through the house to enter Bilby's accounting room.

The agent was often out at this time of the day. He liked

to head to the George Inn in town, drink brandy, and then go off and do things that she knew gentlemen were inclined to do. He had quite a reputation in this area of the world.

"I had no idea you were such an affectionate person."

She whirled around and spotted the very man she was thinking about. Her skin prickled with alarm. "I beg your pardon, Mr. Bilby?"

"You are on very good terms with the new stable man," he said, filling the doorway, blocking any escape, though he stood with nonchalance.

She forced a smile, even as her insides churned. "He's a pleasant fellow."

"Pleasant?" Bilby mocked, crossing into the room, eyeing her up and down in a way that she had never seen him do before. He had made her uncomfortable on previous acquaintance, but he always kept himself distant.

She swallowed. This felt different.

"Yes," he began, his gaze narrowing as he let his eyes linger on her bosom. "I saw the way you mounted that stallion with him the other day and rode about. Very vigorous, my dear, very vigorous."

She wanted to take a step back, but she would not. She would not show weakness. She knew what it meant in the world when one showed weakness. It opened one to attack, and she refused to allow herself to be vulnerable before this man, this man who liked to be difficult. And ruin the lives of those around him.

She'd never been concerned before. Her mother owned a shop, after all, and was able to do enough work to keep them independent of needing Helexton entirely. Though she garnered wages doing work here at the house, they could scrimp by if they had to.

Bilby crossed through the room, his stride slow, straining his breeches, and he unbuttoned his wine-colored coat, as if he was overarm. "Perhaps," he said, "if you were as sweet to me as you were to the stableman, we could reduce your rent or find something that would be acceptable to you. You're pretty enough that I might even reward you with the title of wife if you please me. You could become the grand lady of this place."

Her stomach twisted. Was he mad? "I'm sorry, Mr. Bilby, are you proposing to me?"

"No, Alice," he said with a lascivious smile. "But I'm letting you know what could be possible if you treat me the way that you treat Summers. I've seen you look at him with your big violet eyes."

She swallowed back bile. She supposed she had looked at Mr. Summers, the earl, in a particular kind of way because he evoked feelings in her she never felt before, but she certainly did not have any of those inclinations toward Mr. Bilby. "I think you have the wrong of it, sir. I have done nothing inappropriate with Mr. Summers and—"

He snorted. "I do not believe that for a moment. I've seen the way you two are together, and that's all right," he said. "A little experience is good for a woman, but it seems to me that since you're open to it, you should consider another offer."

She scowled at him, anger bubbling in her stomach. "What the blazes are you talking about?"

"I assure you, he shall not be here long," Bilby warned with an air of satisfaction. "I've already written to the earl and let him know what a terrible decision he's made. The man is spending money hand over fist. He should be gotten rid of post-haste. Also, he's far too friendly with the servants, the boys, the housekeeper. He clearly is not professional and should go back to wherever he came from."

She wanted to laugh, a panicked laugh albeit, at that. Mr. Bilby was going to fire the earl.

He took another step toward her. "Yes, you are very

beautiful, Alice. I've always thought so, but I kept myself apart because, well, I should try to have some respect for the ladies on the estate. And I do have respect for you, my dear, but I think an arrangement would be a very good idea now that I know you are amenable to attention."

She narrowed her gaze, her hand going for the pestle on the table. "*Amenable to attention*," she repeated tightly.

He crossed toward her and lifted his hand, clearly intent on caressing her.

She grabbed the pestle. "Step back, sir."

He laughed. "Or what? You're going to brain me? You would go to jail and I would have your mother evicted from her shop."

A stone dropped in her gut. "You can't do that," she bit out, though she knew it was true he could, if not for the earl. And she couldn't let on that she knew him.

"Oh, but I can. The shop is on Helexton land. Which means I control that land. Your mother doesn't actually own the shop, my dear. You know that, don't you? You *lease* it."

She stared back, horrified. But she had something that Bilby did not know. She had the Earl of Enderley and she'd never be evicted. Her mother would never be turned out, not with Felix on her side.

"Now, now, be amenable and all shall be well." He leaned toward her again.

She brandished the pestle. "I *will* brain you, sir, if you take another step forward."

He laughed again, clearly thinking she was jesting. "I like a bit of fight, and it's good to protest," he said. "One mustn't seem too easy."

He stepped forward again. She didn't want to kill him. She didn't want to go to jail, so she raised her foot and stomped on his as hard as she could, bringing the heel down.

The man's face turned purple as he let out a yelp. "You

horrible wench!" he cried, then hauled his hand back as if he was going to belt her across the face.

Before she could retract herself, a pair of large hands grabbed Bilby, hauled him back, and threw him across the room.

"Get away from her," Felix called, his voice as hard as a whip cracking through the air.

Her heart pounded with overwhelmed relief. "Felix," she breathed.

"Are you all right, Alice?" he asked, his stern gaze still locked on Bilby.

She nodded, though her insides spun with the fear from a moment before. "Nothing happened," she said. "He was simply—"

"I saw and I heard," Felix growled. "Now, sir, get up."

Bilby managed to get himself up off the ground.

"Go," Felix declared, his formidable body crackling with fury.

"You can't tell me what to do," Bilby whined, shocked to be so confronted.

Felix drew himself up. "I can and I will, and I think that my ruse is done."

"What the bloody hell are you talking about? Get off this land," Bilby ordered. "You are fired."

Felix began to laugh slowly, but it was a cold, frightening sound. She had not seen this side of him before. He always seemed so kind, so full of joie de vivre. This was different. Right now, Felix looked as if he could tear Bilby apart and make certain no one ever found the body.

"You, sir, are going to be out of a position and out of a position for a very, very long time," Felix said, his voice low and steady.

"You're delusional," Bilby called out. "The earl will soon hear of what you've done. You attacked his land agent."

Felix took a step forward. "I *am* the earl."

Bilby laughed again, thought it was brittle now. "Don't be ridiculous."

"I'm the Earl of Enderley," Felix said with a frightening calm now. "And I wrote those letters to you. I hired myself. I chose to stay with Mrs. Wright and her daughter because they're far preferable company to you. And I have been watching you, sir, for the last month. It has been most edifying, everything that you've said and everything that you've done. Do you like living in my house?"

Bilby shifted uncomfortably. "You are lying. This is not possible."

"It's very possible," Felix countered. "I know what you have been up to, and if you do not go now, I will make certain that you are put in jail for a very long time. I still might do it. After all, I'm to call on the magistrate later this evening and have port with him. I'm sure that we could find a way, he and I together, to see you on a ship to Australia. I think that would be a very good place for a man like you."

Felix then took his signet ring out of his pocket and put it on his finger.

Bilby paled, his eyes going wide as he recognized the symbol.

"Yes, you're in a great deal of trouble, Bilby," Felix intoned. "I think you should turn around and go. Collect your things and don't ever step back in this house again. And if you ever come near Alice Wright, I promise you that you will never see England again."

Bilby began backing out the door. "This has to be a trick," he said, and yet he clearly understood that he had lost. He retreated through the door and scurried away.

Felix stood for a moment, his body taut with anger before he blew out a long breath and turned to her. "Are you all right?" he asked again.

"For a moment, I thought you were going to kill him," she admitted, her whole body vibrating both with alarm at what happened and relief at what had not.

"For a moment," he said gently, cupping her cheek, "I thought I was as well. I don't want anyone to ever make you feel like that again, Alice," he ground out. "I will drag them through fire."

His proclamation vibrated through her, and in that moment, something deep within her longed to claim him. Claim him as her own. For if he would face hell for her, surely heaven awaited them?

But now that Felix had Bilby, he would go back to London. Back to his old life. And though he had made her promises, she had no idea what was to come next.

Chapter Fourteen

"You are the earl?" Mrs. Wright asked, agape.

Her children were running about her wildly, shouting, whooping for joy, and paying absolutely no attention as they ate their lemon ices. He had brought them to the center of the village and purchased sweets for everyone.

"Yes, Mrs. Wright," he admitted, relieved to at last be able to do so. "I felt compelled to tell you before I confessed it all to everyone else, but the rumors will be confirmed soon. After all, I have fired Mr. Bilby, and he does not seem to be a man who will take things well or with grace."

She blinked, still clearly amazed. "But *you* are the Earl of Enderley."

"That is correct," he said with a smile.

"And you own Helexton."

"Yes," he affirmed. "I realize it is a bit of a shock."

"And my daughter knew?" she queried, swinging her gaze to Alice.

"Yes, Mama," Alice groaned. "I am so sorry that I kept it from you, but the earl asked me to. You see, he was very convinced of the import of him coming here and letting no one know who he was as he did his work."

Mrs. Wright began to nod. "I see, I see, but still, this is quite a great deal to take in." She arched her brow and pinned him with an assessing stare. "You're a very good liar, sir."

"Thank you," he said carefully, for he knew she was still on the fence about him at present. And in truth, he was a terrible liar. If not for Alice's help, he would have never succeeded in his investigation before someone found him out. "Though I should not probably give thanks for it, your daughter does not think so. She had to take me well in hand. I do train men in lying, though, Mrs. Wright. As spies."

She let out a rough laugh. "Surely, I have not had an earl under my roof all this time! I can scarce believe it." She paled. "Your promises—"

"I promised you only one thing," he said.

"Oh?" she asked, blanching, clearly afraid he had lied about many things.

He took her hand in his and assured, "I did not lie in all the things that I said. I will absolutely help your son, Robert. You will not have to fear any boy as clever as that shouldn't be going to university. I will happily pay his college and university fees. I will also ensure that he has a tutor, and I will be writing a letter of recommendation for him."

Mrs. Wright's eyes filled with tears. She blinked, lifted her hand to her mouth, and let out a laugh of disbelief. "My goodness," she said, "it is as if a miracle has walked right into our lives."

"Yes, Mama," Alice agreed brightly. "And on that note, there is something else I should like to say."

Just as Alice was about to open her mouth and, he hoped, declare her intention for her dreams and going to London, a voice shouted, "Mrs. Wright, Mrs. Wright, your shop is on fire!"

Alice's eyes flicked wide, and she whipped around toward the voice.

The look on her face nearly crushed the air from his lungs before he and Mrs. Wright turned as one to the alarming declaration.

The crowded village began to let out cries of distress. For fire was a dire threat to everyone if it got out of control.

As they spotted smoke in the distance, Mrs. Wright's hand dropped from her mouth. She stared for a long moment, clearly at a loss.

Alice rushed to her, holding her upright. "Oh, Mama. I am here."

But then Mrs. Wright and Alice showed how strong they were, their spines straightening, a mirror of each other.

"We must stop the fire," ordered Mrs. Wright with surprising authority.

They all began to run without focus, and Felix called out, "Go to the well! Get buckets! Start a chain!"

The crowd took their heed and swung their attention to the task.

The moment he realized they were listening, he charged down the lane to the house.

Alice and her mother, with her brood, were right behind him.

"Is everyone out?" he yelled, contemplating the need to rush in to the already blazing building. "All of the children?"

"Yes," she shouted over the din. "All of the children came to the village with us."

"Do another head count," he ordered as he eyed the leaping flames swallowing up the ancient shop with dread. "Make certain that no one snuck back in the house."

With that, he darted up to the building and watched as smoke billowed from it, trying to decide if it could be saved.

It was too late. He did not know who had done this, but

they knew how to set a blaze. The fire was already crackling through the ancient thatch roof.

He let out a curse. This was wrong. This was horrible.

Mrs. Wright stumbled as the sight clearly gutted her. "My home," she cried. "My home with Charles."

He took Mrs. Wright gently into his arms, and she sobbed against his shoulder.

"I am so very sorry, Mrs. Wright," he soothed. "We must get the fire put out so it doesn't go up to the village."

Before he could say another word, the men of the village, and women, too, had taken up his call. They already had a long line of buckets going, splashing water onto the fire.

Soon it would be stopped, but the suffering would not.

And though it took countless buckets, the fire did indeed go out, leaving a black husk and smoldering ruin.

Mrs. Wright's legs began to collapse. He pulled her upward again, taking care, and then he heard a disdainful whisper to the side.

"Serves her right. She's probably a witch."

He whirled around. "Who said that?" he ground out, and given his stance and the tone of his voice, a few in the crowd stepped back.

"Mrs. Wright is a great woman," he declared, furious that anyone would cast aspersions at such a moment. "She has shown me so much kindness. She's allowed me to stay here while I investigated Mr. Bilby so that I could discover that the man is absolutely corrupt. Many changes will be happening on my lands."

There was a murmur of surprise over the crowd.

"I'm the Earl of Enderley," he announced, "and this woman and her family are under my protection."

There was another set of whispers, and he wondered then if he'd just made a serious mistake. After all, no doubt, many people had seen him and Alice together, but there was no going back with that. He was going to protect Mrs. Wright and her family.

And soon, he would take Alice away where she could live without judgment.

"Now, let us show her how much we care about her," Felix finished. "How much all of her help has meant to this village."

Then, to his delight, there was a round of applause.

"Anything we can do, Mrs. Wright?" a woman said, coming forward. "You eased my pains after the birth of my Georgie. I don't know what I would've done without you."

Another man came forward, clasping his cap over his heart. "And when I hit my head, Mrs. Wright, it was your assistance that healed me."

Another woman stepped forward, her mob cap dancing. "And when my Johnny couldn't stop coughing, it was your syrup that helped him."

Soon the entire village seemed to be coming up and around to offer Mrs. Wright support.

"We shall not let anything befall you," another man assured.

Mrs. Wright nodded, swiping tears from her cheeks. "Thank you. Thank you, my friends," she said. "It is too much."

"Mrs. Wright," Felix said gently, "you will come and stay at Helexton with me. And, of course, your family."

"At the house?" she said, gasping.

"Of course," he replied, thinking there could be no other option. "Until we can find new quarters for you."

With that, he took her, Alice, and the children away from the crowd. But then he hesitated... The village needed to know. They needed to know his power and how their lives were going to change.

"I am the Earl of Enderley and own the land upon

which this village stands. Any doubts will be removed by my solicitor. I am to take up residence now, though not for long, at Helexton." He drew breath, wishing the villagers to understand his support of them and that opportunities would return. "The house is woefully understaffed," he said. "Anyone who is interested in a serving position should see the housekeeper. I plan on hiring at least twenty people. Helexton must come alive again, and I hope that all of you will be of assistance."

There was a moment of shock, but then he could feel it. Despite the fact that Mrs. Wright's house had just burned down, despite the fact that Mr. Bilby was corrupt, there was hope coming out of the darkness.

He would not allow anyone who had tried to bring this town such darkness to succeed. He would stomp it out. It was the mission of his life, after all, to end the darkness of tyranny.

It did not matter if it was France or a small village of an estate he owned.

Felix led them back up to Helexton, in through the front doors, and up through the foyer.

The housekeeper bustled forward, her keys swinging over her dark skirt, and there was a decided smile upon her usually tense features. "You're... My lord," she exclaimed with shock and pleasure, "we have just heard the news. It is an honor to have you here. I had a sneaking suspicion it was you, just from the questions you asked me."

"Well, you're very clever, Mrs. Brooke," he said. "So I am not at all surprised. Mrs. Wright's house has been burned down, and we must find a place for her and her children to stay. Do you think that you would be able to do that? Something that will make her very comfortable and show her how much we appreciate all that she has done for the village."

Mrs. Brooke blinked for a long moment, no doubt

surprised that a villager would stay in the house. Yet, as any good housekeeper would, she took it in stride. "But of course, we shall, my lord. I shall make certain all the servants treat them with kindness. And in regard to the shop, I don't think a villager did it," she said tightly, her eyes hardening. "I know some people say things about Mrs. Wright, but I just don't believe it was one of them."

And then he swallowed. "You know who it is, don't you?"

Mrs. Brooke folded her hands. "I cannot know, my lord, because I did not see him, but Mr. Bilby collected his belongings and was saying some very venomous things about making you suffer and making you pay." She let out a disgusted sound. "And he has seen the amount of time that you spent with the Wrights. It would not surprise me if—"

"A parting gift," he concluded.

Mrs. Brooke nodded.

It was tempting to let his shoulders sag, but there was too much to do. "Will you take care of everyone, then, Mrs. Brooke?"

"Of course I will. Come, Mrs. Wright," she urged. "And your children, we must get you all settled. There shall be baths to rid you of the smoke and good food."

With that, Mrs. Wright, in a daze, went upstairs with her children.

Alice stayed with him in the foyer.

"Thank you," she said. "Your kindness is—"

"It is not kindness," he broke in. "It is necessary. It is my duty." Anger at himself rattled through his body. "The way I spoke to Bilby... I was rash, and this caused it—"

"You did not do this," she cut in, stepping so close her boots brushed his. "You are not like him, not anything like him. Don't say such a thing. He is a villain, and you, sir, are good. You help people. You would never, ever be responsible for something like that."

"Even good people can cause harm, Alice," he returned, unable to lay down the burden of guilt.

She was quiet for a long moment, then locked gazes with him. "I need you to understand, Felix," she said. "Bilby was vicious. He hurt people whenever he could, and you protected me and you're protecting my family now. Do not ever say it again that you caused this. You have *rescued* us from this, and that is a very different thing indeed."

He nodded softly, though it was damned difficult to heed her words. "And your dreams?" he asked at last. "Are you going to take me up on them?"

"I don't know if I can," she admitted as tears shone in her eyes. "Mama, she needs me."

"Darling," a voice said from the stairs.

Alice whipped around.

His heart slammed in his chest. How long had Mrs. Wright been standing there?

Mrs. Wright slowly descended the stairs, looking surprisingly strong. "What dreams? What have you arranged?"

Alice's face paled. "I thought you were upstairs, Mama."

"I was, but I wanted to thank the earl and…" Mrs. Wright swung her gaze back and forth between them. "My dear, what is this about?"

Felix wanted to reply. He wanted to smooth everything over for Alice, but he knew that she had to say it herself.

Alice cleared her throat, visibly steeling herself to her confession. "The earl has arranged for me to learn perfumery at Madame Clémence's in London. He will find me a place to stay, and I shall be able to do what I've always longed to. But I don't want to leave you," she rushed. "Now is not the right time. I shall stay."

"No, my dear, you must go," her mother declared passionately and drew herself up, as if fortifying herself to hold her ground.

Alice's mouth dropped open. "But Mama, the shop? You must be in such a state."

Her mother gave a firm nod. "All the more reason to leave here, my dear. I do not want you to stay in this small town." Mrs. Wright glanced to Felix with an approving nod. "I'm sure it shall be a wonderful place again. But I came here because I loved your father, Alice. I chose this instead of a bigger life, but I do not want you to choose without even knowing what you are capable of. So you must take what the earl is offering and go with him."

His admiration for Mrs. Wright only grew at her clear love for her daughter and her ability to set her free.

"I trust," Mrs. Wright added, eyeing him, "that you shall take good care of my daughter and assure that nothing befalls her. Isn't that right, my lord?"

He inclined his head. "I promise that I will ensure her success."

Mrs. Wright gave him a strange look then, as if she knew that he wasn't exactly promising what she asked. But perhaps she thought it was something even better.

She smiled at them. "Yes, I can see the way of it. And the future for her. Not through tea leaves or crystal balls, but I have an idea of what is to come. I think it shall be very good, indeed."

He wondered at her mother's strange words about the future. They reminded him of Mr. Perkins's comments, but he shook that thought aside.

"Do you truly believe in me, Mama?" Alice said, her eyes still shining with tears, but this time with an expression of joy.

"Believe in you, my dear?" Mrs. Wright breathed, her gaze filling with love. "You could conquer this whole world if you would but allow yourself to."

Mrs. Wright crossed down, took her daughter's face gently in her palms, and kissed her cheeks, one then the other. "I shall wish you the best of luck out in the world. And I do not believe anything can stop you."

And Felix swore he would make certain that Mrs. Wright was proved correct.

Chapter Fifteen

Felix refused to take any chances with the safety of Mrs. Wright, her children, or the estate.

He hired four Bow Street runners immediately. They had arrived, now, and were going to be guarding the estate for the foreseeable future.

Several others would be looking for Mr. Bilby. Felix had already notified the local magistrate, over a brandy, that Bilby would be a wanted man. Brandy, he found, always made it possible for a magistrate to understand exactly what was needed of him.

Sometimes the magistrate was a local lord. And in this particular case, Sir Blake was happy to be of help to an earl.

After all, he might one day wish to come to court, and Felix would be happy to introduce him to all the right people.

Bilby was going to be tracked down and, if Felix had his way, deported. Some might wish to see him hanged. But Felix would not sit as judge and jury on that particular case. Even so, he was not simply going to let the man go.

Mrs. Wright and her children would be protected; that was

what mattered. The shop would be rebuilt. He had promised himself that. The village would be returned to the glory it had known before Bilby had taken charge and siphoned all of the funds. And his estate was going to be beautiful and full of life again.

He was certain Mrs. Brooke would see to that. She seemed a very capable woman who had been living under the thumb of the land agent.

He had left the boys in charge of the horses, for the time being, but had already hired someone from New Market to come down and run the stables. It had been a great flurry of work in a short period of time, but he was a master of flurries of work in a short period of time. It was what made him so very good at what he did now.

And as the coach headed back to London, he was sitting across from the woman who had inspired so very much of it. He wondered how different it would've been if he had not stood in that lavender field and she had not told him to get his hands off her flowers.

He was exceptionally glad he had touched her lavender, and he was exceptionally glad that they had tumbled to the earth, and he was very glad that she had taken him in hand.

Now it was his turn. He was leaving her world, and she was entering his.

She sat on the bench opposite him, tense, her eyes locked out the coach window as if she could take it all in. She looked both excited and terrified. He supposed it was the correct combination of emotions, but he wished he could take away all her fear and tell her that all would be well.

As the coach pulled into the inn, for it was a good, long journey from Cornwall to London, she let out a sigh. They had been traveling for two days. On previous nights, he'd taken separate rooms for them.

He kept everything polite and correct, but he could not

stop thinking about the conversation they'd had as she taught him how to use a mortar and pestle. Would she take him up on the offer of education, not just as a perfumer, but an education of life?

He wanted it very much, but he wasn't going to push. She'd been pushed already by a villain, and that's not the sort of man he could ever be.

The coach rolled onto the cobblestone yard of the inn, and he gritted his teeth and held his breath. He would take as much of Alice as he could get. As much as she would allow.

The moment the coach rolled to a stop, the door opened and he climbed down. As he looked around, a wave of dread crashed over him.

It was a busy place. The season was starting. He'd been so consumed by his skewering of Bilby and his growing intimacy with Alice, he'd not taken that into account.

People were returning to the city in waves. Suddenly, he realized he might have made a terrible mistake. It was a bit different further out in the country, but this close to London? Great families were coming hurriedly to take up residence in the city before the most important balls could begin.

It was entirely possible that there would be no room. He was an earl, and that would give him some sway, but many people booked these rooms for weeks or sometimes months in advance.

There were several coaches already filling the area. Horses filled the stables. And workers were bustling to and fro with fruits and vegetables, bread, luggage.

Felix winced. It was tempting to have Alice wait in the coach, but they had to find somewhere to stay, even if it was in the stables. The next inn was not for some miles, and it was dark. Traveling at night this close to London was not wise.

Highwaymen were rare, but they were still a reality. And whilst he knew he could protect her, things could still go wrong. One couldn't control everything, not even an earl.

His insides churning, he held his hand out to her.

She slipped her fingers into his and carefully came down the unfolded coaching steps. With her simple clothes, she should have looked as if she might be a servant of his, but the way she carried herself, the confidence in her posture, the beauty of her face? That suggested something else indeed.

So far, while they had been traveling together, he had not felt the need to explain anything to anyone. He did not have to worry about her reputation, nor did she. She was not a young lady who was about to be thrust on the marriage mart; she could do whatever she pleased. And she was never going to be a middle-class wife.

She did not have to worry about the concerns of others. She could be as eccentric as she chose. She was going to be a perfumer, after all. And those kinds of people often thrived on having a rather eccentric backstory. He was happy to help her grow it.

Perhaps being the great amour of the Earl of Enderley would be a wonderful entree in society. She could claim that it was her scent that had drawn him to her; and it wouldn't be entirely a lie.

Ladies would clamor to duplicate such a story.

"My lord, my lord," the innkeeper said with an apologetic air as he bustled out, wiping his hands on his apron. The man looked absolutely frazzled. His hair was wild about his face, and from here, Felix could hear music and laughter coming from the inn.

No doubt, many people were drinking ale and eating their dinner.

"There is no room, is there, good sir?" he asked, fighting a sigh.

"I am Mr. Davis," the innkeeper replied. "It is an honor to have you, my lord. And an earl is always a boon. But you are correct; the inn is very full. All of my good rooms are taken." The man's face creased, perplexed at the idea of dispelling such a man. "I'm not sure where I shall put you. The stables are even full, my lord. But I suppose…"

"Is there not a very small room you might be able to squeeze us into?" he asked, hoping beyond hope. "If I have to, I could sleep in the coach."

"That would be ridiculous," Alice said with a grin. "Sleep in the coach? You barely fit in it as you are."

He laughed, a half groan.

She pursed her lips. "I could sleep in the coach, I suppose. I am smaller."

"Do not be ridiculous in turn," he teased. "We are perfectly capable adults."

"Oh," the innkeeper said, "are you not…" And then he coughed, attempting to recover from his near faux pax. "I do have one small room, meant for a single traveler of less importance. I would never usually offer it to an earl. Will you be able to bear it, my lord?"

"We shall bear it better than not sleeping at all," he informed good-naturedly.

"Very well, then." The innkeeper gestured for them to follow. "Please come along with me. And please, please do not be too disappointed with the poor man who gives you such a lowly thing. It is my honor to try to help you in any way I can. I know on good authority that the inn down the road is also full. It is that busy season."

"Of course it is," Felix said swiftly, wishing to put the man at ease. "I wasn't thinking. I usually travel by myself. And I'm not in need of luxurious accommodation or even a full room if I must."

The innkeeper nodded, then led them in.

It was a veritable symphony of sound. People laughing, people cheering, people drinking, eating their dinner, having political discussions, and talking about Napoleon.

There was little chatter about the latest fashions, since ladies were in the private rooms.

They headed up the stairs, the floorboards creaking. Mr. Davis led them up through a winding passage, down another hall, turning a corner, passing lit sconces, and then he stopped before a simple panel door. "This is what I have."

Davis swung open the panel.

It was a small room, indeed. Some might have argued that it was a closet. But there was a bed in it and a chair and good blankets and a window, small, though, overlooking the courtyard. "This will do admirably," Felix said. "Could you please send up wine, bread, and cheese? Perhaps we shall come down later for dinner, but both of us are exceptionally tired. We've already been traveling for a few days."

Mr. Davis nodded. "Of course, my lord."

And with that, Mr. Davis backed out of the room and shut the door.

"I will take the floor," he said. "Never you fear."

Alice grinned at him. "The floor? I still don't think you'll fit. Not with the chair and the table."

"Well," he ventured, "I suppose I could put the chair and the table outside the room."

He turned about and nearly hit his head on a low beam.

She waggled her brows. "There's that optimism again."

"Indeed," he said. "What is life without optimism? If I had not told him that a room of any kind would do, we would be in a deleterious state."

She clapped her hands together and announced, "I don't see why we can't fit on the bed together."

He looked at her, amused. "I don't think it a good idea, Alice."

"Why ever not?" she protested. "If I sleep pressed up against the wall, you could sleep on the edge. And I think you would have a bit of room for your leg. And you could put the chair close so you could prop your foot on it."

He let out a bellow of a laugh. "You have quite the mind for organization."

"One must problem-solve," she said cheerfully. "It is the only way to get by."

"Indeed." He knew that she'd had many problems to solve over the years with so many brothers and sisters and a mother who needed her. "We shall give it a go," he agreed. "But, if necessary, I'll just throw a blanket down and curl up. I've slept in worse places."

"Have you?" she asked, her brows rising.

"Oh, yes." But he wasn't about to go through the list of strange places he had slept over the years.

She stared at the bed again for a long time and then turned and looked back at him. "Perhaps…" she said softly.

"What?" he queried, his breath hitching in his throat.

"Perhaps I am being overly optimistic," she said.

"Why do you say so?"

She bit her lower lip. "Because I have been very close to you these last three days. And…"

"Yes," he asked, his entire body suddenly alert to her— and the bed.

"It has been the hardest thing I have ever done, to stay apart from you. And now I'm going to spend the whole evening pressed to your side. I don't see how I shall resist."

Heat flared through him. "You don't have to resist."

• • •

The room in the inn was so small they could scarce move without bumping into each other.

Alice was grateful. She had been wanting this for days, and now there was no excuse not to indulge. She wanted to know him fully, totally. She wanted to embrace passion because surely passion would help her become a great perfumer. How could she understand seduction if she never experienced it?

Yes, she needed to know the bliss in tempting another person.

Now, she wanted to know what was on the other side of that temptation, and as she slipped toward the bed, she gazed up at him.

"How do we even begin?" she asked softly.

"Like this," he murmured, and he took her into his arms. He stared down at her, his gaze hungry. It was as if his gaze was a physical thing, awakening her body to desire.

He was slow, and that slowness drove her wild. His fingertips trailed deliberately up her arm, over her shoulder, and then he cupped her cheek. He tilted her chin back with his thumb and forefinger.

His eyes searched over her face and studied her lips. Then, with his lids half closed, as if he was already lost to his own desire, he lowered his mouth to hers. That slow dance he had shown her before? She gave herself over to it, allowing him to draw her into that intoxicating dream.

Felix seemed to lose all hold or control at their kiss in the small room. His breath grew ragged. "I've dreamt of this every night," he rasped.

His hands went to her bodice. He made short work of the laces at the front, and then he helped to slip it down, quickly followed by her chemise and stays.

He backed her slowly to the bed, then eased her down upon it.

It was so tempting to try to cover herself, but he was looking at her as if she was a goddess, and she wanted to revel in the power of that feeling.

In the way *he* made her feel.

Felix sat on the edge of the bed, then delicately began to slide his fingertips between her breasts...he stroked the curves, then traced each of her ribs. He teased over her stomach, then swirled back to claim each nipple. He lowered his head and kissed her breasts, taking those hard peaks into his warm mouth.

She arched against him, shocked that such a kiss could make her feel so very much. Then he raked his mouth downward, over her hips, to her thighs. He worked his way toward the soft inner side and gently parted her legs. As if he had all the time in the world, despite his ever-growing hungry intake of breath, he slipped his fingers into her most delicate place.

She could not breathe. She could not think.

Keeping his gaze trained upon her visage, he circled his fingers, slow and soft at first, but then he began to increase the pace.

It was shocking what he was doing, and yet it was also the most delicious thing she'd ever experienced. She'd never known the bliss of a body contracting, rippling. It was a revelation.

And when he gently slipped his finger deep into her core, she let out a note of surprise, which came out a hum of pleasure.

"Do you like that?" he asked.

She nodded against the pillow. "I want more," she confessed.

It felt so strange to admit, but it was true, and with Felix, she always wanted to tell the truth.

"As do I," he rumbled. He whipped off his coat and shirt.

She studied how beautiful he was, the perfect muscles of his pectorals, the way his abdomen tightened, revealing a series of muscles that trailed down to his breeches.

He stripped the remainder of his clothes quickly, his

movements eager as he joined her on the bed.

She was shocked at the sight of his sex. For she had never seen a man like him before, and it was quite something to behold.

Thankfully, she knew what was to come next, as she was not raised in entire ignorance like some girls. Growing up in the country did help.

Felix laid down beside her, then stroked between her legs again, soft and promising. That feeling began boiling in her anew. She tossed her head and clasped his arms, holding tight, half afraid she was going to totally come apart.

And then her body did shatter, pitching her up, flinging her over and over again into ecstasy. In that moment, she felt completely vulnerable, completely undone, her heart open.

Felix eased himself atop her, gently positioning the head of his sex at her core before he rocked against her.

He thrust forward, and her body tightened. For a moment, she wished to push him away, there was such a sharp pain.

He held still, bracing on his arms. "Are you all right?" he asked, his voice shaking.

She nodded but clenched her teeth.

This was surprising. She had not expected it to hurt so much, but no doubt he was fairly large. Much to her relief, he began kissing her again, softly, slowly as if he could pull her out of the pain.

She began to soften at his hot kiss, and as his sex delved inside her again, this time a little moan came from his throat.

Under his tender administrations, her body adjusted to him.

Letting out a long exhale as pleasure began to burn through her again, she wrapped her arms about his shoulders and gave herself over to it.

Felix began to pick up the pace, his body pumping, his hips rocking against hers. He teased her delicate spot between their bodies again until, at last, her eyes flared open.

And this time, the power of her release was so intense she could not stop herself from crying out his name.

Felix lowered his mouth and swallowed it in a kiss, then he tensed against her body with a groan, joining her in ecstasy.

Chapter Sixteen

Alice wished beyond all wishing that she could stay with the earl.

She knew no one in London. She was completely adrift in this city, and it was a city that was as vital and as shockingly large as the ocean, surely.

The power of it reminded her of the waves that pounded the shore of Cornwall. Only it was a very different power. The cloud of coal smoke that had hung over the city had given her pause.

Felix had not been joking about the air he breathed being without superiority.

Was she truly to live in a city in which there was not a breath of fresh air? And yet the capitol loomed like a jewel. Glimmering with promise.

True, it was perhaps an unpolished stone. She thought of how diamonds came from coal. It was dirty, there were too many people, the noise was a cacophony, horses were everywhere, as were the leavings of said animals, and people darted to and fro.

The streets were crowded, choked even. Young boys and girls, women, men, they sold wares everywhere one looked.

She turned her head this way and that when they had arrived in the city, listening to the cries of every possible thing that one could purchase.

They'd wound through the streets, leading through the great city until at last they had come into a much nicer neighborhood with beautiful brick houses shoring up from the ground. The pristine houses lined the streets. Beautiful coaches raced up and down the roads.

People promenaded along the pavements in bright, stunning clothes.

"Is this where you live?" she asked, agape.

"No, actually, it's not," he informed her. "This is a good area of town, a very good area, but my house is close to Green Park. This is much closer to Bond Street. This is where you want to be, and I own the property that you'll be staying at."

She blinked. This was where she would live? This wondrous place? She had expected a rougher but acceptable place.

"This is it," he said, glancing out the window.

She stared up at the beautiful townhouse with its blue door. "Do you ever live here?"

He smiled. "I have spent time in it before when my tastes ran to simpler living, before I wanted to fully step into the life of an earl, but now it shall be yours."

"But surely I'm to live in a rooming house!" she insisted, her mind a tumult as she tried to make sense of all of the excitement unfolding before her.

"I will not have you in a rooming house at the risk of others," he said. "It is simply unacceptable. Not after what happened with Bilby."

"Nothing will happen to me," she protested, even as she felt a rush of relief at his kindness.

"Perhaps not," he allowed. "But I wish you to live a good life where I can make certain you are safe. I did promise your mother."

She nodded, but then an alarming realization struck her. "I understand, but I am to live alone."

"Does that bother you? I would've thought that after all those years being surrounded that a bit of solitude might—"

"I'm very grateful." She smiled, her insides tightening. She did not want him to think she was afraid or rude.

"Then let me take you up," he said.

He descended from the coach, guided her down and then up to the blue door.

It opened without him knocking.

She smiled to herself as she recalled him lingering before Helexton House, waiting for the door to be opened.

A man in livery greeted them.

"Hello, Stevens," Felix said brightly. "This is to be your charge, Miss Alice Wright. She is a budding perfumer, here in London to make her mark and her name, and we shall help her to do so."

Mr. Stevens nodded. "Miss Wright, it's a pleasure to take care of you. We shall ensure that you have everything you need."

"She will need many things," Felix said quickly, heading in. "She will need an entire suit of new clothes, new shoes, and of course tutors."

She balked. "Why shall I need a tutor?"

"You don't want to be a shop girl, do you?" he asked carefully. "You wish to be more."

"I do wish to be more," she agreed, the words right and yet novel in her mouth.

"Then you will want tutors in the way of society," he affirmed. "You are very intelligent, Alice. It will not take you long. Soon, you shall be the master of London. Once you know exactly what you're about, you shall open your own shop. I'm sure of it."

She beamed at him, so thrilled by his encouragement and his confidence in her. "Where is everyone else?" she asked, realizing how large the place was. "Where is my room?"

Mr. Stevens tilted his head ever so slightly. "This is all yours."

All hers.

She gazed about. There was a long hall with ivory-painted walls, beautiful paintings upon it, and a polished table. She took a few steps forward, then looked to her left. There was a drawing room with green watered-silk wallpaper. The furniture was made of delicate wood and ivory silk. There was a marble mantelpiece with a beautiful clock upon it.

"No," she whispered. "Surely, this is not for me."

"It is, Alice," Felix said, crossing to stand just behind her. "This is the life you belong in."

She blinked. He thought she belonged in this luxurious life?

"Now, I must go," he said. "I have an appointment. I promised a friend of mine that I would check in on him. He lost his wife a few months ago, you see, and I try to take care of him."

It seemed to her that Felix took care of a good many people. And she wondered who it was that took care of *him*.

"Then you must go," she said, though she dearly wished he could stay. For all of this was new, despite the excitement. "And I will go to J. Flores in the morning. Is that correct?"

"Indeed. You have your letter of introduction, and I've already written to them. So you will be most welcome."

She nodded, swallowing back her fears. "Thank you."

And with that, Felix strode out the door, leaving her alone with Mr. Stevens and her new house. Her own house...

"Your lady's maid is upstairs, ready to take care of you

and give you a bath so that you can be prepared for the morrow," Stevens said simply. "Your meal shall be served within an hour. And if you need anything else, it will be arranged."

"I see," she said. "None of that is necessary. I'm perfectly capable of taking care of myself. Mr. Stevens," she said, "do *you* need any assistance with anything?"

He blinked, astonished. "Are you trying to take my position, Miss Wright?"

She coughed as she realized the implications of what she'd said. "No, of course not. I'm sorry."

Stevens gave her a kind smile. "Miss Wright, it is my pleasure to look after you, and it is very kind of you to inquire. I can see that you're new to London and this particular life, but it is also clear to me that the earl admires you very much. I have known him for many years, and he likes to help people. If he has brought you here and he has secured this invitation for you, and me to look after you, he wishes you to thrive. And so I shall help you in that."

"Thank you," she replied, for what else could she say? And she was grateful.

"Come, let me take you to your room." The matter now settled, Mr. Stevens led her up through the quiet house.

It was stunning. She was in awe of it. In many ways, it reminded her of a miniature version of Helexton, but the truth was it was far too quiet, silent.

Even with the sound of coaches racing along the road.

All her life, she had been surrounded by the laughter of children and her mother's voice, and abruptly she realized she was going to be alone.

Very alone.

Would she like it? She did not know.

A great wave of homesickness washed over her, and suddenly she wished she was with her mother, eating her mother's toast and cheese, helping to feed her siblings.

Then after dinner, they would drink her mother's fragrant fruit tea. A treat that always soothed them in the evening.

She longed to be around the table, having conversations about her brothers' and sisters' day, learning what they had done, what fields they had gone through, what creeks they had played in, what birds they had seen.

She would have none of that now.

She was letting all of it go, and she feared she had made the greatest mistake of her life.

"Miss Alice," Stevens said, "this is your lady's maid, Judith."

Judith crossed to her and gave a quick curtsy, her starched cap immovable atop her red hair. "How do you do, Miss Alice? It will be my pleasure to take care of you. Now, come let us get you ready."

"Thank you," she said. "But what may I do this evening?"

Judith paused at that. Clearly, she did not know. "Whatever you would like."

She swallowed, and then an idea sparked to life in her thoughts. "Can I do anything?"

"Of course...within reason," Stevens said, wary.

And then suddenly she knew exactly what she wanted to do this evening because she was not going to spend a whole evening by herself staring at the walls. The silence would strangle her.

"Do you think I could go to Bond Street?" She longed to see the excitement of London's world of perfumes, fabrics, and where the best shops in England resided.

Mr. Stevens and Judith exchanged a quick glance. "If that is what you would like to do, we can arrange it."

"Good," she said firmly. "It's most certainly what I would like to do."

"Come then," Judith said. "We must get you bathed and

dress your hair, and I shall send out for a ready-made gown." Judith gave her a quick, assessing look. "And from the look of you, I can tell exactly what size you are. Will you send out word, Mr. Stevens?"

He nodded. "It shall be done in a trice."

Even as her insides raced, Alice beamed.

Felix had said that she was one for adventure, and that's what she was going to be. She would not hold herself back. After all, she had chosen a world full of wonders getting into the coach, staying in the inn, coming here, and she was not about to throw any of that away. Against all odds, she was in London! Her dream was really coming true.

She was going to seize it with both hands and live boldly and fully.

Chapter Seventeen

The cricket ball sailed past Felix's head and banged into the club's wall.

"We're going to get banned," he groaned.

The Duke of Tynemore hoisted his cricket bat over his shoulder and gave a jaunty grin. "Not with the fees I pay."

It was true. They both paid astronomical fees to belong to their club. But even so, cricketing inside had been banned ten years ago after the incident with Lord Bellfield. The man had gotten falling-down drunk and then managed to knock over a bust of the king and bashed through five windows.

Since then, it had been considered bad form to take to the halls and practice cricket when boredom rose.

But the weather had been appalling the last two hours, pouring down rain, and frankly, he and Tynemore had no wish to box against each other.

They were evenly matched, and neither wished matching black eyes.

It was of course possible that a ball could crack out his teeth, but such a thing was unlikely. He and Tynemore had been playing cricket together since they were small children sent away to school.

"So how have you been keeping since I saw you last?" he asked the duke carefully.

"Oh, very well. Very well, as you can see," Tynemore said, brushing the question off. He turned to the side, positioned his bat, and gave Felix another look, which suggested he should pick up the ball and throw it again.

Tynemore's dark hair fell about his forehead as he focused.

Felix picked up the ball. It was imperative to check on his friend often, and he had not liked being away. Tynemore had not done well after the death of his wife, and one could hardly expect him to get on quickly.

Still, Tynemore used good spirits, jokes, and banter to try to show everyone that he had somehow survived it without being absolutely destroyed.

Felix knew differently. He'd seen his friend's grief. Tynemore had not been able to keep it from him because he had been there the day his wife died.

He'd watched it, the light go out of her eyes and then his. It had been a terrible accident.

She had been climbing in the peaks, lost her hold, and fallen. It should have been nothing, but she'd struck her head upon a rock.

She had not risen again.

How Felix wished that his friend did not always put on such a merry mask, but everyone had their tools to make it through hard times.

"Right," Felix called. "Again."

He hauled back his arm, aimed, then let fly.

The Duke of Tynemore, who was excellent with his bat, hit the ball, and it rocketed again toward the back wall.

"Good show. Good show," Tynemore called. Then he

paused, readjusting his hold on his bat. "Now, is it true?"

He tensed. "What exactly?"

Tynemore cocked his head to the side. "You've arrived in town with a wench?"

"She is not a wench," he growled out.

Tynemore's eyes danced, clearing getting some amusement out of ribbing his friend. "She didn't work in a tavern or some such?"

"No," he gritted. "She is an herbalist, and she's from the country."

"Ah, a country girl," Tynemore said with a knowing sigh.

"Yes. A country girl," he admitted through gritted teeth, sensing where this could be heading.

"So a wench," Tynemore said with a wink.

"You are being difficult on purpose," he retorted. "You told me you did not wish to box, but the way you are going, I'm going to come over and pop you one in the face."

Tynemore laughed. "Now I know you like her very, very much, indeed."

"Of course I like her," he rushed, unable to deny it. "She's skilled, she's interesting, and I brought her here to pursue her dreams."

"That's not the only reason why you've brought her here," Tynemore said. "Is it? Is she your mistress?"

"No, she is not my mistress," he denounced, wondering why the devil his friend was being so damned irritating.

Tynemore paused, looked at him, assessing him, and then said, "She's your lover, then."

He refused to reply. Unfortunately, the silence was a good answer.

"She is my friend," he declared.

Tynemore gave him a strange look. "That is even more dangerous. You always swore you'd never fall in love."

"I'm not going to fall in love with her." He huffed out a

breath. "She's my *friend*."

Tynemore was silent for a very long time. "My wife was my best friend."

Felix's ire died a swift death.

"Yes, she was," he said softly. "But this is different, old boy. We want very different things. She is on the path to becoming a perfumer, and I'm an earl."

"I see," Tynemore said sadly, as if he had hoped that actually, he might be falling head over heels for the *wench*. "So it is class alone and her wish to be a merchant artisan that keeps you two apart? Otherwise, what would hold you back?"

A muscle tightened in his jaw. "You know I have no desire to wed someone I have affection for."

"Yes, and I still think it's ridiculous," Tynemore said, bending over, tapping his bat to the ground. "Come on. Again, again."

Felix snatched up the ball from the ground, eyed the wall, and let out a groan. There were already three dents in it, but Tynemore was good for all of it. And as long as they didn't truly destroy anything or hit a servant, no one would say a word.

Otherwise, Tynemore might grab a brandy bottle and drink himself under the table. Again. It was something he had done several times of late. No one said anything because he was a duke, people loved to drink, and his wife had died. Everyone was rather understanding, so if he caused a bit of destruction with a cricket bat and a ball without actually breaking everything apart, the entire club would look the other way.

Tynemore was a good man, a strong man, a capable man, and he and his wife had been the most powerful couple, driving things in society toward good.

All of that died with her. But he hoped his friend would

pick his charity work back up again at some point.

"When do I get to meet her?" Tynemore asked.

"She's busy," he said swiftly, having no desire for Alice and Tynemore to meet, at least not yet. She needed some time to settle in first.

"Busy doing what?" Tynemore inquired.

"She starts her work tomorrow at Madame Clémence's. That's where she'll learn to be a perfumer."

"I don't understand," Tynemore ventured, his brow furrowing. "She's your friend. You've brought her here, and she's going to go to work? Why don't you just give her money for a shop?"

"She wants to learn a new skill," he said with a shrug. "Surely, you remember what it's like to learn something."

Tynemore threw back his head and laughed. "I learn things every day. I just don't know why you wish to make her life hard."

"I'm not making it hard," he explained. "I've already set her up with a place to live. She will have clothes, servants to look after her."

"And she's not your mistress?" Tynemore drawled.

"No, she's not my mistress," he countered, narrowing his eyes. "I owe her a great debt."

Tynemore pursed his lips. "What did she do for you, then?"

"She helped bring that rogue Bilby down."

Tynemore tsked. "What a devil he proved out to be. I read your letter."

"I'm glad. I didn't know if you'd have time, what with all your banter and witty repartee." He palmed the ball, tossed it in the air, and prepared to throw. "Have you been leading several salons as of late, getting into philosophical debate?"

"It is the only way to pass the time," Tynemore pointed out. "It is great fun to rile them."

"Just as long as you don't get called out in a duel," he warned as he threw the ball.

Tynemore hit it with ease again, and it rushed through the air, cracking against the wood.

The truth was Felix did sometimes wonder if his friend would be called out by some fellow who took offense to the way Tynemore liked to prod and poke holes into people's verbal arguments.

Tynemore suffered fools with a tongue-in-cheek sort of cutting commentary. Usually the person who was at the end of it did not know it was even happening. And so things passed without consequence, but Felix feared one day that someone was going to be insulted, refuse to take it, and not care that Tynemore was a duke. Or in a fit of rage, forget he was a duke.

Tynemore, of course, was capable of handling himself in a duel, but Felix hated the idea that something might go amiss and he'd lose his friend, just because the man was run ragged with grief.

"I want to meet her," the duke insisted, and then his gaze brightened. "I could arrange it and she could be introduced to society. A perfumer! Though they are usually Parisian. Oh dear, she's a shopkeeper, isn't she?"

He fought the urge to roll his eyes. "I didn't realize you were such a snob."

"I am not a snob," he retaliated with melodramatic offense. "I'm suggesting launching her, and you know the sort of people I invite to my house."

"Intellectuals," he pointed out. "Artists, but apparently you have disdain for a girl who grows flowers and turns them into something beautiful."

The Duke of Tynemore let out a sigh. "Forgive me. You have a point."

And before another ball could be tossed, a footman

crossed into the room bearing a silver tray. "My lord, there is a note for you."

He frowned. "I wonder what the devil it could be."

Tynemore shrugged.

Felix crossed quickly and took up the note, then read the words swiftly and let out a groan. "Bloody hell, I need to go."

"Trouble in paradise?" Tynemore asked.

"Not exactly," he began, surprised at how pleased he felt to be needed by her, even if she didn't know it. "But I have to make sure everything is going well."

"Can I come?" Tynemore asked, a mischievous tone to the question.

He swung his gaze to his friend. "Of course you can't. This is between myself and Miss Wright."

The duke's lips twitched. "I still can't believe that her name is Miss Wright."

"It's not spelled like that," he insisted.

"No," Tynemore agreed. Even so, he clearly found the whole thing too good. "But don't you think perhaps the fates are laughing at you? I mean, surely when one meets someone called Miss Wright—"

"I never should have told you that," he said, closing his eyes and pressing his hand to the throbbing at his temple.

"You are my dear friend. Of course you should," Tynemore corrected. "Besides, I need things to rib you about. You're far too serious."

"I am not," Felix exclaimed.

"Well, you have been of late," Tynemore warned. "So go on, then. Go help out your young woman. Is she going to go out on the town? She is, isn't she?"

He winced. It was true. The note said she was heading out to Bond Street. What was she thinking? She did not know London at all. But then he realized it was he who was the idiot here.

He had left her, assumed she would rest and go to bed and not be entranced by the excitement of it all. He should have set something up for her, taken her himself, but he hadn't lied to her.

He really did want to make sure Tynemore was all right.

And given the man's nonstop, blitheful banter, he was fairly certain Tynemore was not all right. He was hiding his pain. And far too well.

"Run along," Tynemore encouraged. "Mustn't have a lovers' quarrel, you know."

"We're friends—"

"Very good friends, I'm sure." Tynemore waggled his brows, then waved his hand. "Go along, go along."

And as he left, he wondered, was Tynemore right? Had they crossed over into the land of lovers? He'd assumed that making love to her would not change their friendship.

He prayed the duke was wrong. For if he was right, he would have to end things soon...or find a new way to play this out.

Chapter Eighteen

This was a terrible idea.

The road was choked. The coach had brought her around to Bond Street, one of the most popular streets in London. She'd had no capacity of understanding what that meant exactly.

Until now.

Much to her chagrin, Felix had arranged for her to have a coach for means of transportation. He had done everything, made certain everything was just right for her, but she had not understood what it truly meant to get into a coach for an evening in London Town and then go to the most exclusive shopping street in all of England.

She had read of it, of course, in books and in stories, and in the news-sheets. But this? The size of it, the mass of coaches attempting to drop off their occupants before the glittering storefronts, was mind boggling.

The idea of going out had seemed delicious because the idea of staying in was unbearable. But now, as she sat here in her new day gown, which did actually fit but felt incredibly odd because it was made of silk, she felt an absolute fool.

She pulled at her fawn gloves, shaping her fingers and arms to perfection, and again felt at odds. She'd never worn gloves like this. This wasn't her life. Her hair was curled beautifully. A bonnet decked with roses sat atop her head, and a ribbon had been tied at her throat.

Her bosom was covered by a beautiful Spencer that matched the rose hue of her gown.

She did not have a companion, and as she gazed about, she realized that there wasn't a single woman out here on their own, except those trying to hawk wears in the street.

This was ridiculous. She was a fool. She should not have come.

But she had wanted… Oh, she did not know. It all seemed ridiculous now.

She leaned toward the door, ready to pop her head out and call for her driver to take her back, when all of a sudden it opened and a large, gloved hand thrust in.

She let out a yelp of alarm.

Was she about to be accosted? Had she done something wrong?

"Alice," said that rumbling, glorious, gorgeous voice she knew so well. "Come down."

She sat frozen on the bench for a moment. Surely, it could not be. How had he found her? But she was so glad he had. And so, heart beating apace, she slipped her gloved hand into his and let him guide her down.

She caught his gaze, and all of her fears immediately disappeared. The crowd vanished, the shouting, the calling, the buzzing conversation, the scents, the sights, the mad dash of it all.

It all fell away as she stood in front of Felix. He towered over her, and his beautiful bicorne hat only made him taller. His black cloak hung over his broad shoulders. A jewel glimmered in his cravat. His perfectly pressed breeches clung to his hard legs. His coat was beautifully cut, and his hair was styled but still a bit wild.

"What do you think?" he said. "Will I do as your escort this evening?"

"You're not supposed to be here," she protested, though her heart danced with joy that he had found her. "You're supposed to be with your friend, taking care of him."

"Oh, I did that," he assured. "And then he insisted I come show you Bond Street."

She gasped. "What?"

"Stevens sent word that you wished to go out, and I thought perhaps you would allow me to join you."

"Allow?" she echoed, her heart swelling at his attention to her. "I was just about to tell the coachman to take me home."

"Are you unwell?" he asked, concern darkening his eyes. "Do you wish to go?"

"No," she assured swiftly. "It's just I realized how ridiculous I was being thinking I could come here by myself."

"It was a trifle dangerous," he agreed, "but so was getting on the horse with me. So I'm not surprised that you've done it."

He pulled her closer and gazed down into her eyes as he held her hands gently.

"I'm sorry that I left you. I should have known you'd wish for entertainment—"

"No. It wasn't that at all. I was lonely," she said, though she hated to admit it. "Felix, you must understand. I have not been alone in my entire life. Not really. Not like this. I've gone to the fields by myself, but I've never spent an evening on my own. And I was terribly uncomfortable. So I thought—"

His face softened as he understood her plight. "Why not come and enjoy the city to ease the quiet?"

She nodded.

"Then it is my honor to introduce you to all of this."

"You have introduced me already to so many things," she reminded, chagrined.

He smiled down at her. "And you to me. Where would I have been without your assistance?"

"It's not the same," she protested, flustered at his admiration.

"It is," he disagreed, not brooking argument. "You guided me through your world. Now let me, as we discussed, guide you through mine. Shall we, Miss Wright?" he asked, presenting his arm.

She could not stop the smile that tilted her lips or the warm feeling of affection that lifted her spirits. "We shall, my lord."

And with that, he guided her forward.

Bond Street was not a wild cacophony. Not compared to her first taste of London streets.

And yet, it was an orchestration of so many varied notes. She'd only seen groups of musicians together once or twice at country balls, but she'd always been amazed at how they could play different tunes and be in sync, coming together to play a greater song.

And that was what Bond Street felt like as she strode down it with her arm tucked into Felix's. He guided her so easily across the pavement's rough bits, puddles, mud, and through the vast, colorful collection of human life. There seemed to be every walk of person about to fill her senses with wonder.

People sold flowers, some were simply promenading back and forth in beautiful, sumptuous clothes. There were people who had servants trailing after them with boxes. Ladies with grand hats and feathers sailed across the street, and gentlemen with cloaks escorted young ladies to and fro.

She could not stop looking about; her head felt as if it was on a veritable swivel. Every moment she saw something new. She felt very much like a child in a pastry or sweet shop seeing each new delight, her imagination coming completely to life, as every moment was revealed to her as one of wonder.

The village shops could not compare to those in the city in any way.

Here, the storefronts were beautiful and decorated, each one showing what they specialized in. Brightly colored ribbons hung in one store. Hats with plumes, lace, and flowers lined another.

Bolts of shining fabric graced the windows of one across the street. Canes, parasols, everything a young lady could wish was on view.

And of course, she spotted Madame Clémence's across the way. Her heart leaped in her throat at the sight of the polished windows and scrolling letters announcing the name of the perfumery.

That's where she would go in the morning. She could not wait. It was tempting to dash across the street and dart in, but she was not going to do that. When she entered, she would go as an invited member, not as someone to gawk.

Now, she wanted to take in the atmosphere of Bond Street.

"Would you like me to take you into any places?" he offered simply. "We can buy as many things as you wish."

"No," she rushed, savoring the feel of her gloved hand resting atop his beautifully clothed forearm. "That is not why I'm here. And while I find that is very kind of you, I don't want you treating me as if I am…"

"What?" he said softly.

She frowned, hoping to explain herself without offense. "Some pet to be pampered."

He choked on a laugh. "Dear God. Alice, I could never

think of you thus. I wish to see joy upon your features. That is all."

She joined in his laughter, relieved. "You've already accomplished that. You brought me to London, didn't you? And you met me here. How did you know I didn't want to be alone?" she said softly.

"Alice," he said, gazing down at her from his tremendous height. "I don't know how I knew it was so important. I simply knew that I had to come and be with you. This is all new to you, and you need a guide. Just like I needed a guide in Cornwall."

"Fair." She grinned at him. "Now, shall we walk about and observe life at its finest?"

He smiled at her. "Whatever you wish is my command."

With that, he led her through the crowds again, and she felt a war within her, one of amazement at the sheer volume of humanity milling about, going in and out to buy things.

But she also felt a strange hungering for home all of a sudden. The swift, piercing nature of it, almost stole her breath.

The wide spaces of the fields, of the flowers, the horses, the village, the weaving streets, her brothers and sisters...and the care of her mother.

This was a never-ending place of consumption. And she abruptly wondered if she had made a terrible decision. She'd come to London to learn the trade of perfumery, with perhaps the idea of opening a shop here. But in a flash, the idea seemed mad, for she felt completely off-foot, surrounded like a bit of wood bobbing in a great sea.

She swallowed.

"Do not be afraid, Alice," he said softly, as if he could sense her inner turmoil. "You are capable of meeting and rising to the occasion of all of this."

"Am I?" she asked, a desire to retreat rattling through

her. "It all seems so very much."

"New things always do. But you must not allow that which makes you comfortable to pull you back and keep you down."

She blinked and stared up at him. "You wish me to be uncomfortable?"

"Yes," he said boldly. "If you want your dreams. But I will be there to help you every step of the way, if that's what you want."

His words raced through her blood and crashed around her heart. He would be there, her champion, believing in her, even when she was afraid.

She squared her shoulders and lifted her chin, buoyed.

"Then I shall dare to be uncomfortable," she said, "because at least I know that I'm not alone."

And yet, in this vast sea of humanity, she wondered if anyone could ever truly feel as she had felt at home with her mother and her brothers and sisters.

All the disappointment she had felt for her mother, for the way she'd given up on her dream? Alice wondered now... Had her mother simply chosen differently? Not less, but different.

Alice did not know. And the only way to find out would be to try, just as Felix was urging.

Chapter Nineteen

"Would you like me to go inside with you?" Felix asked her.

She had barely slept last night after their adventure to Bond Street. She had thought all night of what this moment would be like. And now as she stood here in the cool air of morning, the light dim with London's murky cloud cover, she felt relieved he had come with her.

"Don't you dare," she warned, poking playfully at his beautifully clothed shoulder. "They shall all think I'm terribly incompetent if you do."

"You?" he countered. "Never."

She laughed, so very grateful for his presence, but it was now time for her to go in alone. They stood together on the busy pavement in front of Madame Clémence's.

"I wish you to have the best of days," he said, pulling her close to him again, though he did not dare to wrap his arms about her in public. It was clear he longed to kiss her right there, but that was not the done thing in society. She knew that much already, but she had so much more to learn about the way of things here.

"I will," she promised, tilting her head back the better to gaze up at him. "I'm going to make you proud of me."

"I'm already proud of you," he said. "Now go in there. And do what you've always wanted to do."

He squeezed her hand and gave her a small, jaunty salute.

She turned and headed up the steps, then opened the door herself and stepped over the threshold into the hallowed heaven of perfume. She gazed around, awestruck. Glass bottles, beautifully labeled with ribbons tied about their necks, lined the counters. The sight took her breath away.

Ladies and gentlemen moved back and forth easily as they sampled the different scents. Several girls and young men dressed in the most beautiful of striped blue uniforms, offered assistance to any who wished it.

She stood still for a moment, not entirely certain where she was supposed to go.

So she took another step forward across the floor inlaid with a mosaic of wildflowers. One of the attendants spotted her, eyed her up and down, and then went around the end of the counter and spoke to an older gentleman, who then spoke to a polished-looking young lady, who then spoke to another lady with tightly coiled hair.

And that lady bustled toward her, huffing. "My dear," she whispered, sotto voce, trying to shoo her toward the door. "I do think you happen to be in the wrong place."

"Oh no," she returned, digging in her reticule for the earl's letter. "This is definitely the right place."

But before she could get it out and produce her evidence, the woman raised her nose and shook her head. "I hardly think so."

"This *is* Madame Clémence's," Alice clarified, her hand now awkwardly stuck in her reticule. "The sign says so above the door."

"It is," the lady agreed, nodding, which caused the soft

collar at her throat to bob. "Of course it is. But you clearly don't—"

"I have an appointment," Alice cut in swiftly, beginning to sense what was happening.

"An appointment?" the lady queried with disbelief, adjusting her apron.

She drew herself up and stated, "Yes. I am to learn the art of perfume-making."

The lady gaped, agog for a long moment, and then let out a laugh before she clamped her mouth down and swallowed the sound. The attendant smoothed a hand along her apron and challenged, "You?"

Alice tensed. She had never been laughed at before. This was new. She straightened her shoulders. "My name is Miss Alice Wright, and I do believe the Earl of Enderley secured my appointment."

The lady's lips pursed at that, and instead of being impressed by the mention of the earl as Alice had thought she would be, she gave her a sly look up and down. "Oh, I see. Is that the way of things, is it?"

Alice took a step forward, propped a hand on her hip, narrowed her gaze, and said tersely, "Look here, you gutter minded fool, I don't know what way you think things are, but I have been growing herbs and flowers since I was three years old, and I know already how to make perfume. So I'd like to know how long you've done such a thing to speak to me thus."

The lady gaped. "Well, I never."

"Clearly not," Alice agreed. "Now take me to whoever it is I'm supposed to be meeting."

The attendant turned around in a flurry of striped blue linen, sniffed, and led the way.

Alice followed quickly, doing her best to appear unshaken. She wasn't about to be left behind. They wound through the packed store and then headed into the back.

"Madame Clémence! Madame Clémence!" the attendant called. "There is someone here to see you."

Madame Clémence, a short woman with silvery hair piled atop her head, suddenly popped out from behind a desk. "Here I am," she said in a thick French accent. "And who is this?"

"Miss Alice Wright," the attendant declared with a hint of iciness.

"Go on, Joanne," Madame Clémence urged with a wave of her hand. "Go on, go back to your work. And merci."

Joanne huffed, turned about, and strode back onto the shop floor.

"My, my, mon chérie," Madame Clémence sighed. "You have done much to put one of my girls into such humor."

"She doesn't think I belong here," Alice said.

"Ah, I see." Madame Clémence shrugged. "Who does belong here, my dear? I certainly do not belong in London, but here I am. I had to leave Paris, and now I live here. You are from Cornwell, I understand? And now you live in London like me."

"My mother was from France," Alice supplied, though she wasn't sure why.

"Oh indeed? Where was she from?"

"Toulon."

"My goodness, that was quite far away from Paris. But your mother, she knew her plants and her tinctures?" Madame Clémence folded her beringed hand before her. "This is what the earl has told me."

"What else has the earl told you?" she asked, curious. "Because the lady out there seems to think that…that he and I…" Her cheeks flamed.

"Oh no, no!" Madame assured quickly. "Joanne has a small mind. I keep her because she knows how to handle rude customers and the worst of the ladies. But you are not a rude customer, my dear. You are here to learn, and I am happy to teach you. The Earl of Enderley is a good man, and he has done a great deal to help those in France who have been left behind. He donates a great deal of money to the cause of my kind and tries to get people out."

"I had no idea," she breathed.

"He's a very powerful man, so it is likely there is much that you don't know about him."

The words hit her like cold water. It was likely that she didn't know very much about him, and yet she shared so much with him.

She'd shared her time, her dreams, and so much more. She swallowed.

How was it possible that Madame Clémence had cut her down to size in a few words without intending to?

"Now, I would put you up in front to learn at first, the way of things here, but as I understand, you already worked in your mother's apothecary?"

"That is true," she stated, but the fact did not feel enough somehow, and she had to keep her hands tightly folded to keep them from fidgeting.

Madame Clémence eyed her slowly, up and down, assessing. "Now, the sort of people you have served, they are very little like the people you will meet here. And we must be honest about this. Country people, they are good, they are wonderful. I admire them. But you will not be selling perfume that costs a fortune to a country person. Still, you are not prepared to go out there, my dear. They will devour you!"

"I have a tutor," she admitted, "and the earl is helping me."

Madame Clémence clapped her hands together. "Good. They will teach you how to handle ladies and lords. They are quite fussy, you know."

"I did not realize," she admitted ruefully. "My interactions with the earl don't seem to suggest that most are."

"He is singular, my dear," Madame Clémence explained. "Most of them are very difficult and very particular. They only want the best, even when they don't know what the best is. But they think I am the best, so they want me," Madame Clémence said with an exclamation of joy.

And in that moment, Alice knew that she liked Madame Clémence. Very much.

"Your dream is to own your own shop?" Madame queried.

"Yes," she said boldly, though the admission did make her nervous.

Madame Clémence's eyes danced with mischief. "You wish to go into competition with me?"

"No," she rushed, horrified the woman might think such a thing.

Madame Clémence laughed. "But if you open a shop, surely it will compete with mine."

"No," she said more firmly this time.

"What do you mean?" Madame Clémence asked.

She drew in a breath and explained her reasoning. "Just because there are two perfume shops does not mean that they need to compete with each other. Is it not possible that we offer very different things, with very different tastes and styles?"

Clémence cocked her head to the side, causing her silver hair to shift. "I like the way you think, my dear, because in truth, this is a very large world, and I think there is room for everyone in it."

"I agree," she said, feeling at ease now and rather overjoyed to work with this woman.

Madame Clémence winked. "I am glad that you agree with me because otherwise I would have to kick you out this very moment."

"My goodness, you are blunt," observed Alice. Perhaps she had something else in common with Madame Clémence.

For had she not been blunt with the young woman out front? She was relieved, for such speech assured her there would not be games and maneuverings employed by her new mistress.

The playful but firm nature of the perfumer filled the air. "Life is too short for anything but being blunt, my dear. Learn it now. You may be blunt with me. And I suggest you be blunt with the earl, but not the customers. They need to be led with artful flattery. Come along. Let us see what you know and what you don't know."

She led her down through a hall and into a long room.

"I want you to take all of these herbs and categorize them and tell me which you think would go well together."

Alice stared at the room. There were hundreds of dried flowers and herbs before her, all in boxes. "I…"

"Do you feel that this is a task you are not capable of?" Madame Clémence queried, eyeing her carefully.

"No, but I think that there may be herbs and flowers here that I am not familiar with," she admitted.

"Wonderful," Madame exclaimed with excitement. "You shall increase your palate and your nose. It is good to experience new scents, but that does not mean that you won't be able to tell what goes together."

"Of course, you are correct," Alice realized, and she drew in a calming breath. She could do this. Indeed, she could. Her mother believed in her. Felix believed in her. She only needed to believe in herself.

"If you have a knack for it, you will be able to tell immediately what notes will marry each other and which notes should get an annulment or a divorce." Clémence laughed.

Alice had never heard another woman speak like this, and she liked it very well.

Madame Clémence clapped her hands together. "I shall leave you now, and then I will join you for luncheon, because everyone should eat a good luncheon. If they do not eat a good luncheon, they cannot make good perfume. Angry people do not make good perfume."

And with that, Clémence bustled out of the room, leaving Alice to her task.

There were aprons hanging on the wall.

Alice took one down, put it over her head, then tied it back around her waist. It looked as if she was to work alone.

She did not truly mind. She was accustomed to that. But more than anything, she wished to please Madame Clémence. And she wished to please herself and prove to herself that she was capable, that she could tell which herbs and flowers needed a marriage, a divorce, or an annulment.

She might also tell which ones were to be friends, which ones were to be lovers, and which were the ones *she* loved best.

She traced her hand slowly from box to box, first gazing upon the colors, gazing at the different flowers. Some immediately leaped out to her eye, bright and beautiful.

Others were more subtle.

She took care with them, because people were so wont to overlook the subtle, small things in this life. But in her opinion, it was the subtle, small things that were the most powerful. Like noticing a man standing in front of a door, waiting for it to open.

Oh dear. The memory...

A smile came to her lips that she could not force away. That's what he did to her, just the thought of him.

Her dreaded heart.

Her dreaded heart was falling for Felix, loving him. How could it not, after all they had shared? After all he had done for her?

And she wondered if her heart and his were meant to be together. And she hoped—even though he had made it very plain that they would not—she hoped that they did.

Chapter Twenty

Alice climbed the stairs of the townhouse, tired but exhilarated. Every day was long, and she had worked very hard these last weeks. She entered the perfumery just as the sun was coming up, and she did not leave it until the sun was almost coming down. She enjoyed her evenings out with Felix, of course, but sometimes she was absolutely exhausted, and she loved when he chose to spend the evenings in with her.

As she gave her things over to the butler, she smiled at him.

"He's here, Miss," he said with a friendly look.

"Is he?" she asked, her body suddenly feeling light.

The butler nodded. "He's upstairs."

"My goodness," she exclaimed, all her tiredness vanishing from her limbs at the promise of spending the evening with Felix. And without another word, she raced up the stairs, eager to see him, to share her day's excitement.

She loved telling him about the things that she was learning, and she loved hearing from him about what he was doing in Horse Guards.

Though he could not tell her much. So many things were confidential in the work of spies.

As she headed into the small drawing room attached to her chamber, she stopped, shocked. He stood at a long table with several things atop it.

He turned slowly to her and smiled.

"What have you done?" she asked, awe filling her.

"Well," he began, looking hopeful but hesitant, "if I'm honest, I have no idea what to give you, and I wish to give you so many things. I could bring you jewelry. I could bring you flowers. I could bring you cake. I could bring you clothes—"

She laughed. "Yes, you could bring me all those things, but clearly you have not."

"I thought this would be better." He gestured to the latest scientific equipment for making perfume.

She was stunned, overwhelmed, and her entire body felt as if it was glowing from his thoughtfulness. Here was everything she would need for the distillation process, of all of the notes of perfume she might ever hope for. The ability to steam, to create heat, to transfer the droplets of water that had been infused with the scents of lavender, violets, freesia, and any of the other earthier notes that would form the base of the perfumes.

She let out a gasp of astonishment. "This is for me?"

He grinned. "Well, it's certainly not for me. I don't even know what to do with most of it, but I asked Madame Clémence what I should get you so that you could practice at home if you wished to create your own samples. And she said this was the best set there was. She looked at me with a great deal of impatience. No doubt she thinks I'm impossible," he said. "But there was also a note in her eyes that seemed pleased you were so excited by the work that you might wish to continue to explore at home. Have I missed the mark? Do you work enough at the perfume shop?"

Home. He kept referring to this place as home... But, she realized, it wasn't the building that gave her a sense of home.

It was him.

"This is not work to me," she admitted. "This is my life, my dream. So this gift is wonderful. I do not have anything like this that is mine. At the perfumery, I must use Madame Clémence's things."

She rushed forward and touched each little piece of equipment, eyeing the glass, handling the different items. The vials. She let out a cry of exultation. "Thank you," she said, wrapping her arms about him.

He gazed down at her, and his face, though filled with delight, had a certain tension to it. Even so, there was a look to his eyes that suggested he was deeply glad to give her something that thrilled her so.

"Did you have a difficult day?" she asked, her stomach fluttering with nerves for him. "You seem..."

"No, no," he assured swiftly. "It's all a part of my work. Sometimes I have to give news to people that isn't pleasant or hear things that are hard, but it is simply part and parcel of what I do. And seeing your joy now?" He pulled her closed and stroked his hand along her cheek. "Well, it alleviates a great deal of the difficulty of my work."

"I'm glad," she said, leaning into him, savoring the feel of his hard body pressed to hers.

She stared at the perfumery set. "I would like to use it immediately. First, I must set it up correctly and then collect the flowers and seeds for the different notes."

Joy laced through her. Oh, the possibilities!

She let out another cry of exultation and grabbed his hand. "It's too late to go down to the market to purchase things for it," she said with a hint of disappointment. "I shall go first thing in the morning before work, and I shall collect all the things."

He held his breath for a moment, then smiled. "Perhaps I have done something I shouldn't. But look."

With that, he went behind another table and brought up a crate of necessaries. "These are all the things that I could find. Various seeds, dried herbs, dried flowers—"

She let out another gasp. "You're so…thoughtful," she said. "Because you could have brought me jewels, but they would not have been precious to me. But this…" She clasped the glass canisters, eyeing each item, each beautiful thing. Each component which had been lovingly created, and she gazed at Felix with wonder. "You know these are jewels to me."

She placed them on the table, then offered her face up.

"Kiss me," she commanded.

His hands roved down her back. "Are you certain?"

"Was that not what you were hoping for?" she teased, desire blossoming deep within her.

"I will always hope to kiss you," he informed, his gaze heating. "But I wanted to see this look on your face. The joy. But if you wish me to kiss you, of course I shall."

"Then do not wait," she urged.

Felix lowered his mouth to hers, passion wrapping them up. She wound her arms about his shoulders, a different thrill now lacing through her blood.

And as he lifted her and placed her on the table, she let out a low moan of pleasure against his mouth.

He kissed her with an unabashed desire, and in his seduction of her body, her thoughts vanished.

He slipped his hands to her face and cupped her chin. Gently, he traced kisses over her cheekbones, then down to the curve of her throat.

The delicious feel sent a shiver of anticipation through her.

He slid his hands to the edge of her skirt, then began to sweep them upward.

She arched toward him. "What should I do?" she whispered.

"Lay back," he urged, his voice rough with hunger.

Her eyes widened, but she followed his suggestion, laying down beside his gift.

The cool table skimmed her back, and she gazed up at the gilded ceiling.

Felix stroked her thighs, first the outsides and then the tender flesh inside. He swirled his fingers over her exposed hips, dancing ever closer to the V between her legs.

Her body ached with bliss and every growing desire for him as a low moan slipped past her lips.

Felix's gaze turned hot as he fixed his stare on her sex. Then slowly, he leaned forward, held her hips fixed with his palms, and then caressed the folds of her sex with his mouth.

A jolt of bliss blazed through her.

As he kissed, and teased, and tossed her body upon a sea of building pleasure, she gave herself over to this man who gave her so much.

She tossed her head from side to side, trying to gain purchase on the table before she grabbed hold of his shoulder, riding the pleasure his mouth gave her.

She knew, deep in her core, a core coiling with desire, that she wanted him not just for this ever-building feeling but because he saw her for who she was and he did all he could for her dreams.

The relentless, soft brush of his tongue over her most sensitive spot drove her higher and higher and then, oh then! He slipped two fingers into her core, caressing her within, and she could no longer hold herself back. The strokes of his fingers, plunging into her, and his lips over her sex sent her over the edge into bliss.

Her body coiled as she surrendered to pleasure. It crashed over her in ripple after ripple, and she cried out his name.

And as he straightened, undid his breeches, and teased the head against her sex, their gazes locked.

In all her life, she'd never felt so at one with a person. Never felt so much.

It was terrifying and beautiful.

Felix thrust deep into her body, and they moaned as one as their bodies united. He rocked his hips, his face transformed by his desire, as he never looked away.

Here, all the world vanished and everything that separated them slipped away.

As if they were one…

And as they both crested into bliss together, it felt as if they always would be.

Chapter Twenty-One

"Madame, please… Madame!" The voice of Felix's assistant, Mr. Merriweather, rang out in the hallway beyond Felix's large office.

He stilled and closed his eyes.

It was never a good sign when Merriweather raised his voice. The man was a column of calm, and yet at this particular moment, there seemed to be a trace of hysteria outside.

He strode to his mahogany door, grasped the golden handle, and pulled it open. Felix strode over the richly woven rug and spotted a young woman, babe in arms, on the point of hysterics, tears streaming down her face.

Her long black gown and dark bonnet sent a sinking wave of sorrow through his gut.

"I cannot believe he is dead. I cannot believe it!" she exclaimed. "I must see the Earl of Enderley."

"Madame, he is very busy," Mr. Merriweather attempted to explain, his spectacles winking in the morning sunlight.

"It's all right, Merriweather," Felix soothed as he strode

forward. "May I be of assistance? I am the Earl of Enderley."

The lady swung to him, and hope filled her eyes for a moment, but then sheer anguish twisted her face, and the babe began crying at her breast from its mother's distress.

"Come with me," he encouraged. "Let me give you assistance. Merriweather, will you please send for tea?"

The man nodded and set off.

Felix took the young woman's elbow and guided her toward his office. He took her over the threshold, led her to the fire, and gently helped ease her into one of the chairs. She looked as if she might pop up again at any moment and begin pacing about, but she gazed down at the face of her baby instead and let out a low moan of suffering.

The infant could not be much more than one year of age.

"I received a letter from you, my lord," she said.

"Did you?" His throat tightened. He didn't want to jump to conclusions, and so he allowed her to continue, even as he feared the worst.

She licked her lips. "In it, you said my John had…"

She could not complete the words, and he winced.

Almost certainly, she was talking about John Falcon, a young man he had recruited who was fluent in French and was a veritable chameleon in his ability to change personalities.

"I see," he said patiently, sitting beside her so that she might feel heard. "Can you be clear about whom you mean?"

She nodded. "John Falcon, twenty six years of age, born outside of London, traveled back and forth to France many times within his youth with his father."

"Yes, I know whom you speak of," he assured. "He was a very good man. I'm so very sorry for your loss."

She shook her head, her dark bonnet bobbing. "I received several letters telling me that John was missing, but suddenly I received notice of his death, and I refuse to believe it's to be true. He cannot possibly have…"

His heart twisted, and he wished he could lie to her, tell her that John was coming back. But John was buried under French earth and would never see English shores again.

"I'm so very sorry to tell you, Mrs. Falcon, but it is confirmed. There are witnesses that saw John die, and his body was put into the earth. Unfortunately, we cannot bring him back to England," he said. "It's not possible with the war going on, but I promise you he was buried with respect."

She stared at him for a long moment. "With respect?" she echoed. "What care I for that, if I never see my John again? He is my sun, my moon... How shall I carry on?"

"Forgive me, Mrs. Falcon. I'm going to be very blunt and perhaps you shall find me cruel. But John is not here. The infant in your arms *is* here now. Though I can see your anguish and how much you clearly loved your husband."

She let out a rough cry. "Yes, of course, my baby is the reason why I get up every day. If I did not, I would not come out of my bed." She paused, and then her face creased with torment. "I must go to work, for I cannot allow my baby to starve."

He'd made sure that she had a widow's pension. It was part of his work to ensure such a thing, but it wasn't much. He knew that.

"You have work?" he asked gently. He could only imagine how hard it was to go to work when wrapped in the mantle of grief.

"I do," she said, her voice weak. "If you can call it that, but it is hard to find someone to care for my baby whilst I work, you see."

His teeth ground at her predicament. "Yes," he said. "I understand. I will do what I can for you, of course."

And he would. He did everything he could for the men who served him, but he had not realized how difficult it was for Mrs. Falcon at present. He should have. It was his business to know. He longed to kick himself.

He would do better.

"I will help you find someone reliable to care for your child," he said. "Someone trustworthy. I understand there are many nefarious people in the city who look after infants, and I would not wish you to feel concerned about it."

"Thank you, my lord. That means a great deal. But that is only the beginning," she protested. "How am I to go on without John? He is my other half. I loved him so much. Loved," she gasped, her voice breaking. "What a terrible thing to say. I love him still. Surely, there is a mistake. Surely he is coming back."

The agony pouring off of her nearly undid him. Felix leaned over to her and held out a hand. Reluctantly, she slipped her fingers into his as she rocked her baby side to side.

"I wish I could tell you that John is coming home, and it is perhaps no comfort to know he died a hero for his country, but he is not coming back."

She blew out a harsh breath. "It is not a comfort to know that he died a hero," she said, then her voice took a mournful but proud note. "Perhaps it is a comfort to know that he died to save others."

"And he did," Felix assured. "John's work was making certain that more people are not killed. I'm very grateful to John for all he did. He helped many men."

"Did he?" she breathed, her voice shaking.

"He did, Mrs. Falcon. You and your child must be very proud of him."

Tears streamed down her face.

It was the danger of love.

He'd seen it far more than he liked, and the truth was it was simply another reason to make certain he never succumbed to it. For he would never be able to do his job properly, never be able to help women like Mrs. Falcon or others like John. Or his country.

He would not be able to help the people of England fight back against a vicious tyrant if he was mixed up in the mire of love, which could tear someone to shreds and leave them incapable of carrying on. He only prayed that Mrs. Falcon would be able to bear up for her child. He had seen grief tear people to ribbons. It struck him with terror, that danger. How he wished he could take it away from her.

All his life, he had been distant. He'd been sent away to school at five years old. He'd never been particularly close to anyone. The Duke of Tynemore was his dearest friend and perhaps now, of course, Alice.

She was his friend, someone he could speak to, share his bed with, but he would never love her and this was exactly why.

Love was one of the cruelest things there was. If something happened to him, he could never do this to Alice. He would not allow her to be torn apart by grief, and if he were to fall in love with her and something happened to Alice? He could not allow himself to be drowned in the black tar of grief. No, he could not let either of them be taken apart, dismantled, unable to live without misery.

No, it was far better to choose stoicism in this life. His parents had been right to send him away to school, to teach him distance, emotional separation. That was the only way he could carry on as he needed, helping many men rather than just a few.

The only way he could ensure the success of the men across the water, who were ascertaining secrets every day, was to shore up his heart.

It would be a betrayal of them to ever allow himself to slip into love. Just as it would be the height of cruelty to enmesh someone else to him.

But he could do everything he could to assist Mrs. Falcon.

He squeezed her hand. "The baby is very beautiful," he said. "He looks like John."

She nodded, a small smile crossing her wan face. "He does. He even has John's personality."

"How wonderful," he said softly, doing his best to bolster her, though his whole body tensed with his failure to protect John. He wished he could keep all his men safe. But war was a brutal master. And safety was never guaranteed. Only hoped for.

"He is the only joy I have," she said,

He nodded kindly, longing to honor John's memory and his sacrifices. "Then we will make certain that this boy is very well taken care of, and I promise you, Mrs. Falcon, you will not be alone. I will personally see to that."

And he would.

He would visit her every week. He would visit the baby, too, and he would make certain that John's death would not be in vain and that his wife would be able to carry on even through her black despair.

Chapter Twenty-Two

"I knew your grandfather, you know, mon chérie."

Alice stopped mid-work. It was the most that Madame Clémence had said to her in the last two weeks. They had been working together almost silently, side by side. Alice had been doing meaningful but uncomplicated work: sweeping up, taking care of the herbs, keeping everything organized, stored, taking care of the alcohol and oils. Making sure that everything was available for ointments, so that when Madame Clémence did her work, everything was ready for her.

It had been a continual activity of standing in wait or peering over Madame Clémence's shoulder or being left to carry out the essential basics.

She was happy to do it, of course. It meant the world to her to finally, daily, be able to do such things. She had done things like this every now and then with her mother, but there had been no consistency in it, certainly not after her father died. It had been like a treat, something brought out at Christmas, to lift her hopes and spirits.

But now it was becoming part of her life, a daily activity,

and she was getting better and better at it.

She'd always been good at making perfume. Her mother had seen to that through the times they had spent together. But now, she was letting it become like a memory in her bones.

Still, Madame Clémence was always quiet, always studious, always passionately attached to her work, leaving little room for conversation, except for instruction.

This seemed almost shocking to hear her speak now, especially of Alice's grandfather.

"How did you know him?" Alice blurted.

Madame Clémence shrugged, but there was a sympathetic light in her eyes. "He was a perfumer, was he not?"

"Yes, he was," she admitted, her breath hitching in her throat, realizing she might learn more about her grandfather. "How did you…"

Madame Clémence let out a tired sigh, but then a smile, one full of nostalgia, lit her face. "You keep mentioning your mother. I remember the little girl running around her father's shop. And I…remember the tragedy of his end. It was terrible, and it was why I no longer was interested in just making perfume for kings."

She shook her head at this admission, stunned. "But everyone in London seems to think…"

Madame Clémence let out a laugh. "That I only made perfume for the most important people in Paris? Well, I did make perfumes for them. But of course! Especially after your grandfather left. They needed someone like me. But chérie, my greatest work was in the upper middle class, in the bourgeoisie." Madame Clémence carefully wiped her hands on the front of her pristine apron and turned to fully face Alice before she continued, "The bourgeoisie long to be like the great nobles. It is not so very different here. They wish to smell like them and to dress like them, of course. It was always been my pleasure to provide until I no longer could."

"What was he like?" she asked softly, her voice nearly breaking.

"Your grandfather?" Madame Clémence's silvery brows rose. "Come, we shall work side by side."

Alice crossed to Madame Clémence and stood by her at the long table, where they began to work with the various beakers.

"I'm amazed to see so many tools and accoutrements," Alice admitted, "instead of the simple, old ways."

Madame Clémence laughed. "Yes, your grandfather was a traditionalist, but I believe that science will change everything, and I am most certainly a woman of science. The old must give way to the new, and there shall be many new additions to the perfume world in the years ahead. Soon, it will allow for many people in the city to be able to afford such delights." Madame Clémence tsked. "Now, so few can, but with the future's opportunities, we shall be able to make perfume that is still beautiful but not quite so dear in cost."

She blinked, trying to make sense of Madame's words. "I don't understand. Don't you wish to make it for only..."

"An exclusive clientele?" Madame Clémence cut in, adjusting her beakers, studying the steam rising in one, adjusting the distillation of the freesia in another. "No, I don't. Why would I want only a few people to have what I make? I wish as many people as possible to enjoy it. And you? Do you not wish to see many enjoy it?" Madame Clémence leaned forward and winked. "You do, after all. I have smelled the perfume on you. Your mother made it?"

"No," she said softly, proud of her own work. "I did."

"You did?" Madame Clémence exclaimed, clapping her hands together. "My dear, it is exquisite. It gives me hope for you."

"Why?" she burst out, her heartbeat pounding at the

comment. "Am I so very terrible at my job?"

Madame Clémence tilted her head to the side, then said bluntly, "No, but you are too quiet and not bold."

Her jaw all but dropped, and she protested, "But I thought you wanted…"

"Yes, of course, I want you to do your work," rushed in Madame Clémence. "But I expect you to pipe up to make decisions and choices."

Before the liquid could begin dropping on the table from a finishing beaker, Alice quickly placed a vial underneath it.

"And what will you mix with a freesia?" Madame asked.

She fought the urge to nibble her lower lip but instead chose to appear confident, lifting her chin. "I think another beautiful scent, perhaps a fruit."

"A fruit?" Madame pursed her lips before she tossed out, her eyes narrowing slightly. "Fig, perhaps?"

Alice swallowed. It was tempting to simply agree with Madame Clémence. But she dug her nails into her palms and dared, "No, fig would be the wrong note."

Madame Clémence's eyes danced as if she had been hoping Alice would disagree with her comment. "You are right. What would be a good note to mix with fig?" she asked.

"Vanilla?" she ventured.

"Yes, very good. And of course, we must have a solid base for the other notes to dance upon." Madame Clémence folded her arms across her crisp apron. "You must get that structure correct or it shall smell terrible."

Madame Clémence blew out a breath. "Now, I could say that all I want is to make perfumes for a few of the great ladies and lords of society, but I want people like you, my dear, to be able to enjoy it. And even you? Well, you are not like others, who do not have the fortune of a mother who knew how to make perfume. Because of her, you learned how to make it, so you can make it for yourself and indulge in such a beautiful luxury. But all of the other people…" Her face grew grim. "It is not possible. What do you think of my opinions?"

She lifted her chin. "I think it's wonderful. I think that perfume cheers one, lifts the spirits. And I think as many people as possible deserve to have their spirits lifted, especially in such times."

"Perhaps…" Madame Clémence's voice trailed off.

"What?" she prompted, wary, half afraid she'd said something amiss.

Madame Clémence picked up a box of dried rose petals. "Do you truly wish to own a shop of your own, or is it the work you enjoy?"

Alice frowned as the question rolled through her. In truth, she'd never thought about the difference. "I've never owned a shop, so I can't possibly know, but I dearly love the work. I always have, since I was small."

She began to pick glass vials that would collect the distilled liquid, so that they might be mixed and layered later.

"Good, mon chérie. Good."

And as if the matter was settled, Madame Clémence turned toward the opposite table. "We shall have to make sure that we have enough alcohol for the base mixture of the perfume," she began. "That is the most expensive, of course. We can also use oil for this new scent, the one I shall introduce for a larger clientele. I want to experiment this week and see if we can create an excellent aroma that doesn't necessarily take the most expensive ingredients. Good ones, of course. We will never stoop to anything that is harmful or foul," she said vehemently. "I only want people to know joy."

Madame Clémence's words filled with an intense feeling that cut through the room. "I have seen so much suffering, and you, mon chérie, I think you have seen suffering, too."

Alice bit the inside of her cheek, stunned that Madame Clémence was allowing such conversation between them. She felt close to the older woman, as if this was the beginning of something far larger than she'd ever imagined.

Alice nodded, at last. "Perhaps that is why I like doing the work," she said. "It comforts me. I don't like being out front in the shop."

Madame Clémence laughed. "Leave that to the other girls, then. They adore it! It is far better than most of the work in this city. But you? Allow this"—she gestured to the room about them, full of the tools to make perfume—"to be your refuge, your haven. Choose that which makes you happy. The work."

Those words filled her with a profound peace. Any fears or doubts she'd had were swept away. This was what she had always wanted. And now she was doing it.

"I will," she proclaimed, feeling that she had found her purpose at last.

Chapter Twenty-Three

Mrs. Prenilla Makebury's Society for the Tutoring of Young Ladies was not at all what Alice had suspected it would be.

She wasn't entirely certain what she had thought would occur when endeavoring to learn manners and how to behave with one's betters, but this certainly was not it.

A confectionary of young ladies pranced about the room, all of them in various shades of soft pastels. It was exceptionally sugary, from soft dandelion yellow to pink peony. She felt as if she had entered a rather eccentric sweets shop.

Still, she was here for a purpose, and she had been here now for several days. Every afternoon when she finished at Madame Clémence's, she came to learn how to treat customers with the respect and finesse they supposedly deserved.

Mrs. Makebury stood, dressed in lavender widow's weeds, festooned with crisp lace, waving her handkerchief as she navigated her way from one lady to the next, improving their gait as they walked in circles.

Alice had been walking in circles now for twenty minutes. It was a miracle she could walk at all, given how poorly she'd been apparently doing it all these years.

The book upon her head was balanced carefully. Her neck was straight, her shoulders were back, and this all seemed like a terrible waste of her time.

She could be making perfumes at present!

Instead, she was watching her posture, and earlier she had spent a significant time conversing about the weather. Also, she had learned how to pour a perfect cup of tea. Over the last week, she'd learned how to dance the most popular dances, in case she had the good fortune to be invited to a dance, which she doubted would ever happen unless it was Felix doing the inviting. She'd learned how to properly use a fan, how to dab a handkerchief, and how to flatter with ease. How any of this was going to help her make better perfumes, she did not know.

"Your face is quite sour, Miss Wright," Mrs. Makebury trilled from across the sunlit room, her sausage curls bouncing about her face.

It was a pleasant face, a kind face even. But it was a face most concerned with the edification of young ladies on how to be cakes.

This was the only way that Alice could think of it. There was nothing substantial here. No, everything was a pastry. And pastries were well and good, but Alice, well, Alice was fairly certain that she was not a pastry at all. No, she was a field of wildflowers and what others might consider to be weeds.

Even so, she continued walking in a circle, attempting to change her face, appear as a pansy, when in truth she felt more like a foxglove.

"My dear Miss Wright," Mrs. Makebury chirped, rushing over, her skirts blowing about her ankles as she fluttered forward. "You must make more of an attempt to give a merry expression. No gentleman or lady shall wish to speak with you if this is how you are."

Mrs. Makebury did not educate the highest ladies of society. No. She was in the habit of teaching young ladies who wished to be shop girls, and she taught them how to behave with customers of a genteel class.

It was a very specific style of education. After all, young ladies of the *ton* had governesses and various other tutors to teach them, brought in to live with the family. Or the young ladies were sent to finishing schools.

"What do you propose that I do?" Alice asked, trying to relax her face, but her brow kept on furrowing, rather like a field waiting to be planted.

Mrs. Makebury tutted and gave a wave of her lace-edged handkerchief. "Well, my dear, allow your lips to soften. Allow your eyes to widen, your eyelids to flutter. And you must look upon your customers if they're the most divine creature in the entire world, as if they're about to say something utterly breathless."

*Oh dear...*she groaned inwardly.

"What if they say something utterly absurd?" she asked quite seriously. "What if they were to ask for something ridiculous? What if they were to be rude? And if they say something unpleasant?"

The words tumbled out of her as she tried to make sense of this new world she had thought she wanted to be a part of. Now, she wasn't so sure.

Mrs. Makebury let out a laugh, one that felt forced and bell-like...as if she had practiced for such moments as this. "Oh, you must laugh, my dear. You must laugh as if it is the most amusing thing you have ever heard and carry on."

Well, that was not how her mother had raised her. It was not how she had spent her time in Cornwall. And it certainly wouldn't do when picking flowers.

All this felt terribly wrong.

She was used to being in back rooms, after all, immersed elbow-deep into oils, flowers, fruits. And in her other hours? Immersed in soil. The fragrant earth a haven for the seeds that would bring forth beautiful plants.

But this, this was something else altogether different. It was artificial and performative. She didn't know how she was going to carry on with this. For surely, it had nothing to do with the making of perfumes.

"Is this truly how people must behave?" she asked bluntly.

Mrs. Makebury blinked. "Whatever do you mean, my dear?"

"Don't you find it a bit silly? All this cheer, all this pretense?"

"My dear," Mrs. Makebury stated. "The entirety of society is built on pretense. And if you think not, well, it is not for you."

Perhaps it wasn't.

She adjusted the book atop her head and kept walking. Mrs. Makebury turned from her and swooshed over to another young lady, tugging at her shoulders.

For the most part, the other ladies about the room were doing marvelously well. All of them had quite pleasant expressions upon their faces. All of them were wearing their pale gowns, their cheeks pink, their hair curled to perfection.

And Alice was rather certain that her own hair was doing its best to burst out of its coiffure. She did try to keep it in proper curl, but it would riot apart.

Then there was the fact that, well, she did like to stride.

Shop girls apparently did not stride.

But she was used to going through the fields, picking her flowers, spending time in the earth. The earth was beautiful. How she dearly loved the soil and its rich components. For soil gave life to healing flowers as well as the pretty ones.

This prancing about seemed, well, entirely unnecessary to the making of perfumes. And it struck her then that perhaps she was on the wrong track entirely.

She was deeply grateful to Felix for arranging this for her. She had made it clear that to own a shop, she'd need to navigate society.

But now, here in London, after spending a great deal of time with Madame Clémence, in the back of the French lady's shop, it was becoming clear to Alice that the idea of actually having to own a shop and smooth the feathers of the upper classes was...well, rather unappealing.

She had no talent for it. And as this thought struck her, her head tilted and the book collapsed to the floor in a rush of pages.

"Oh dear," Mrs. Makebury called out as if it was the most horrifying occurrence in all of the world. "Oh, my dear," she said. "What am I to do with you?"

She stared at the fallen book for a moment, then knew that her labors were meant for something else entirely. Certainly not the fluttering of lashes or skirts. "Absolutely nothing. But I thank you for your endeavors."

And with that, she bent down, picked up the book, and carried it to Mrs. Makebury. This wasn't the place for her, and she wasn't entirely certain if it ever would be. No, she belonged with the essences and oils and distillation of things. Not in the sugarcoating of them.

Chapter Twenty-Four

The days went by in a flurry of events. Every morning, Alice eagerly went to her work, and every evening, she eagerly went back into Felix's arms.

The nights! The nights were a revelation. Every evening they went somewhere different: they went to the theater, they went to poetry readings, they went to literary salons. He took her to eat beautiful food, and they went to Vauxhall Pleasure Gardens.

He'd taught her to dance and guided her about the floor.

Fireworks had exploded in the air, and she felt as if they were exploding inside her as well. It was heaven.

She had never been happier in her life, spending each moment, as soon as she was done at the perfume shop, with Felix. She was shocked he had so much time for her, but it seemed as if he had as much desire to spend his evenings with her as she did him.

And this evening seemed no different.

Except this evening, she was full of trepidation. They had been invited by the earl's friend, the Duke of Tynemore, for an event.

Event was the only word she could think of to describe it. It was not technically a dance, nor was it a ball, because it was outdoors in the summer air.

She was dressed beautifully. A gown had been made for her at one of the shops on Bond Street, one of the most exclusive ones. It was a blue silk confection. The fabric caressed her skin with the same sort of whispering touch that he used in the evening when they laid before the fire in each other's arms.

It was cut low. There were mere scraps of fabric that tied about her shoulders in gentle bows. The hem was embroidered with small pearls and beautiful irises.

It shimmered with silver-shot thread.

Her hair had been coiled by Judith into the most beautiful pattern at the top of her head, and a single large curl teased the curve of her bosom.

Butterfly pins had been put into her hair, and they shimmered with jewels, because, much to her shock, he had been determined "that she would be the most beautiful woman there."

And that required jewels, it seemed.

He had brooked no refusal when he had brought them over in a red leather box and handed them to Judith to put in her hair. She wasn't entirely certain how she felt about all of this grandeur for herself. She was so accustomed to a simple life that in many ways, she did not like it. All she wanted was to be a perfumer. Not a grand lady. A simple life was best. One that did not interfere with her flowers and fruits and recipes.

But she loved how he looked upon her in her finery. And that? That was pleasurable.

It was perhaps the only thing that made it possible for her to sit next to him in the coach, trying to stay calm, clutching at her fan and tugging at her gloves.

"You will be fine," he said. "You will be adored."

"So you say," she said, realizing she had no great wish to be adored by society. Unless it was as a perfumer. "But I am about to be presented to your friend and people that are not of my class. I shall make a muck of it," she said.

"You shall not," he said as he locked gazes with her. "You have never made a muck of anything in your entire life. You're going to win them over easily."

How she longed to see what he saw. But she was a country girl. A goose among swans, surely! They would sense how deeply out of place she was.

He took her gloved hand in his and raised it to his lips before he warned, "But what you must not do, whatever you do, is try to be one of them."

"What?" She frowned, trying to understand.

"Do not try to be like them," he insisted, running his lips over her knuckles. "Just be your interesting, remarkable self and they shall adore you."

She drew in a breath and closed her eyes. "This is madness. I should ask you to take me home."

"Imagine if we had not gone to the opera," he pointed out.

She let out a bemused groan. "Don't do that! You like to throw my fears in my face and remind me how once I did the thing I was afraid of, I loved it."

"Well, it's true," he said, smiling.

"Yes, yes, I understand. The stallion, the opera, and now this," she said.

She'd loved Mozart. That night she'd seen *The Magic Flute*. She had thrilled to her very core at the notes the orchestra had played and the arias the singers had sung.

She'd not experienced anything like it in her entire life, and she supposed that was going to continue on with him.

Every day she was experiencing things she had never had the opportunity to know.

A footman opened the coach door. There was no hiding now.

Felix climbed down, and he offered his hand to her.

Boldly once again, as always, daring her to go further and do more with her life. She drew in a long breath, took up her skirts, and followed him down in her perfect, new slippers.

When she stepped upon the woven rug that led to a pavilion, she blinked. Were they in a fairy land? It certainly seemed so. Lanterns danced on wrought-iron hooks. Music filled the air, and people in diaphanous clothes, shimmering with gold and silver, surrounded them.

"Where are we?" she asked, trying to take it all in. The wealth was almost unimaginable. Servants maneuvered about in red-and-gold livery, balancing silver trays covered in crystal punch cups and flutes.

Jewels glittered everywhere like stars in the firmament.

"The Duke of Tynemore's London home on the river." He leaned in and whispered, "We've come round the back way, to the gardens."

"He has set all of this up to meet me?" she choked.

"He likes to put on a show, you know?"

"I did not know," she said.

But she had read about Tynemore in the newssheets. The man was constantly entertaining, and he was also constantly lobbying in parliament. His parties were renowned, or at least they were before his wife died. Even she knew about that.

She had not realized that the duke was who Felix had been speaking of when he said he needed to go to his friend. It was a tragedy the whole country had heard about, and even mourned, because Tynemore's wife had been a beloved duchess who everyone looked up to.

She had actively campaigned for reform, she had helped

people, and she had opened orphanages and fought for education for the poor. She'd also glimmered like a star shooting across the night sky.

Now, she was gone and her husband was left behind, and said husband wished to meet Alice.

She could only imagine it was to ascertain whether she was good for his friend or not. And for that, she immediately admired the duke.

They headed along the runner. There were peacocks everywhere, footmen passing trays of wine, and as soon as they came to the top of the runner, she realized there was a man announcing names.

He boomed out, "The Earl of Enderley and Miss Alice Wright."

With that, they descended into the crush of people toward the various tents that had been put up.

It was a party to introduce her, but there were hundreds of people as far as she could tell. In a way, she was relieved. Surely, she'd be able to fade into the colorful background?

An orchestra was playing by the man-made lake. There was a fountain in the center of it, a sort of Neptune with a trident, and water gushed up from a horn that he seemed to be blowing.

The entire thing was opulent. Trees bloomed all around them. And rose bushes had been brought in and arranged in elaborate sculptural shapes.

Couples danced upon the pavilion floor, like jewels winking in the sun.

"Come and dance with me," Felix whispered against her ear.

She licked her lips and glanced about. "Do you not wish to introduce me to your friend first?"

"Oh, never you fear. Tynemore will find us."

And just as Felix was about to lead her onto the floor,

someone cleared their throat. "Will you introduce me to the country girl?"

She tensed. "Country girl" was said with affection. There wasn't a hint of snobbery to it.

And so she turned to face the man. "How do you do, Your Grace? It is an honor to meet you."

"Is it?" he drawled. "Thank you. Truly, the honor is mine. You have captivated my friend. And I never thought to see that."

For a moment, she could make no reply, she was so stunned.

"Oh, stop it, Tynemore," Felix groaned.

"It's true," Tynemore intoned.

"Well, in all events," she rushed, doing her best to seem confident, "I must thank you then for inviting me to this party."

Tynemore leaned in, waggling his brows. "Oh, I'm sure you have already deduced this is entirely for me to spy upon you, my dear. Now, away with you, Enderley. She is all mine now."

Felix looked at her carefully. Clearly, he would argue with his friend.

"Now, you keep in your barbs," he warned Tynemore. "I know you love to cut, but she's capable of cutting back."

His friend grinned. "Good. I'm glad to hear it. Dance with me, Miss Wright?"

She knew it was meant to be a question, but it almost sounded like a statement, a foregone conclusion. Which, she supposed, it was. "Of course," she said.

Alive with nerves at being so close to Felix's dearest friend, she allowed him to take her on stage.

She had been learning to dance; it had been one of the things that he had insisted upon in the evenings over the last weeks.

He had taught her himself, and it had been full of laughter and kisses, as well as tumbling into each other's arms.

Now, she could waltz, she could do a reel, and she could do a polonaise and a few other country dances. Luckily, this one appeared to be one of the simple couple dances that would be easy to perform and did not require a great deal of touching.

They took up position on the floor.

To her consternation, everyone was watching. She supposed she shouldn't be surprised; after all, she was a simple miss, and he was a grand duke.

Alice curtsied as the music began. He bowed ever so slightly, then they began the elaborate pattern of the dance, easily weaving back and forth.

"You have entranced my friend," the duke observed.

"He has entranced me," she replied easily.

"A witty answer," he said, inclining his head. "But, you understand, I must protect him."

"From me?" she queried, pivoting as her stomach dropped at his intimation.

He gave her a rueful smile. "A winning young woman from the country comes to London and suddenly knows good fortune? Well done you, my dear. But I must ask you, how do you plan on using him?"

"Using?" she echoed, her body tightening with offense. "My goodness. You do not hold back, do you, Your Grace?"

"I find there is little point in wasting time," he agreed.

"I keep meeting people who feel the same," she mused, trying not to crackle with anger and recall he was trying to protect Felix. "And I agree with you, so I shall tell you this: I am not using him. He is not using me. We are friends."

He rolled his eyes.

"We *are* friends!" she insisted, her insides shaking with indignation.

"And more," he returned.

She nearly stumbled at that, and she bit back a curse, wishing she was as nimble on her feet as she was with herbs.

She cleared her throat. "How do you possibly…"

"It's the way you look at him, my dear. You look as if you are the cat that has had the cream."

"How very boring of you to use such a cliche," she returned, refusing to be intimidated.

"Cliches are cliche for a reason," he whispered. "He looks at you the same, if it comforts you. And what I want to know is if you're going to make an honest man of him."

"What?" she gasped.

This time, she did trip. Not because he'd startled her with his question, but because she had thrust her foot into the hem of her gown and she feared she would rip it. A gown that had so much fabric she was unaccustomed to it. Her own gowns were simple. For she could not afford extra yardage nor such delicate cloth.

Much to the duke's credit, he caught her with ease. "I have overwhelmed you so easily?" he teased.

"My toe is stuck in the hem of my gown," she confessed, trying not to panic.

And then the duke gave her a sympathetic smile, knelt down before her as everyone stared, and disentangled her as if it was the most normal thing in the world.

He stood again, twirled her under his arm, and began leading her back and forth. "I want to know if you're going to marry him."

"No," she said tightly, beginning to feel embarrassed. "Of course I'm not going to marry him. Besides, he hasn't asked me."

"And if he did ask you?"

"No," she said fiercely. "He has been very plain about the sort of woman he wants for a wife, and I have an entire profession planned."

"Pity." The duke sighed.

"Pity," she echoed, confusion rattling through her.

He nodded. "I think you would be perfect for him."

She swallowed. "How could you know such a thing? We have known each other but a few minutes."

"Perhaps, my dear, but he has written to me about you over the weeks, and we have discussed you. And I've seen the change in him. How could I not want him to be happy? You make him happy. I hope that you both see reason soon."

"Why in good God's name are we not seeing reason now?" she exclaimed.

"You're both utter fools," he said, twirling her under his arm again. "Both of you think you don't need love to survive this life. He wants to marry for an heir and practicality, and you want your profession. You know," he said, "you could have both."

She stared at him. "No. I have seen what can happen."

"You saw what happened to whom?" he prompted.

"My mother," she confessed.

"Ah, but you know your mother's fate is not yours, don't you?"

She blinked, his words thundering through her. "What do you mean?"

"Just because you're worried you might become her doesn't mean that you actually will." He gave her a surprisingly kind smile. "It is a story you are telling yourself in your head. And I urge you, my dear, I urge you beyond all things, create your own story. Do not live out the lives of others. And do not make decisions because you are afraid. You will regret it for the rest of your life."

With those rather shocking words, the music ended. He turned from her, gave her a bow, and led her back to Felix, leaving her completely unsettled.

Chapter Twenty-Five

She had been asked to dance every dance. It was delightful to see her so admired, for all the people who danced with her were interesting.

And she was reveling in it.

Most of the guests were philosophers and intellectuals, people who were ready and eager to change the world, artists, theater makers, musicians. People that the Duke of Tynemore found important, people that he was trying to lift in society. Of course, there were other people like him, other powerful people who enjoyed Tynemore's unique company. This was an exclusive party, after all, and it was elaborate.

Balloon flights were now happening, lifting up into the sunset. Soon, he wagered there would be fireworks that could easily compete with Vauxhall.

He would not put it past his friend who now approached with champagne in hand.

"I ought to murder you," he drawled.

Tynemore gave a mock look of horror as he stood beside him. "Why ever would you murder me? I have done you a great favor."

"This is not a favor, my friend," he gritted. "You have done something mad."

"And what is that?" Tynemore said, his eyes dancing.

Felix willed himself to patience, though he longed to throttle his friend. "I know you said something to her out on that dance floor."

"Look at how happy she is," Tynemore observed. "What could I possibly have said that would warrant murder?"

He glared at his friend. "I saw the way that she was looking at you when you were speaking with her. What mischief were you planting?"

"Oh, nothing," Tynemore said, quite innocently, sipping his champagne.

"Do not lie," he countered. "You are not particularly good at it."

"I am far better at it than you are, and you know it," Tynemore drawled. "It's all the artful dancing I have to do with politicians. You mostly have to deal with the people at Horse Guards. They're difficult enough, but none of them are as difficult as silly old lords who don't want to vote for important things like ending slavery on sugar plantations."

He nodded. "I admire your tenacity in the face of adversity. I just have to worry about Napoleon taking over Europe."

"That is most certainly its own sort of problem," Tynemore said. "And I'm very grateful that you're trying to stop him. But to hand, you would be far better at it if you were happy, and she makes you happy."

"I agree. I'm happy in her presence." He drew in a breath, admiring the way she glided across the floor. "She's very busy at her work."

"You're going to lose her, you know."

He swung his face toward him. "What the devil are you

talking about?"

"Look at how everyone adores her," Tynemore mused. "She's simply too marvelous for words. I like her. Everyone likes her. She's beautiful. She's capable, and she has a talent. She's going to rule London, or at least she'll rule the demi-mondaine."

His smile died, and his jaw tightened. "I will be happy for her when she does."

"Will you?" Tynemore challenged. "Or will you be kicking yourself because you let her get away?"

"I don't think that we should be discussing this," he growled, stunned by the strange emotions churning through him. When had he become so...volatile? Had he not always been a master of himself?

"What else should we be discussing?" Tynemore countered mercilessly. "I have few people that I intimately care about, and I want to see that you are with the right person."

"I do not need help in this."

"Oh, fine," he said with a dramatic sigh. "I shall leave you to it. No doubt she shall find someone else to admire her when you are done, because that is what you're saying, isn't it? You're going to be done at some point or the other?"

"It's a natural progression of many relationships," he gritted, even as the words turned to bitter gall in his mouth.

Tynemore gave him a withering look. "I have no more patience for you."

And with that, the duke headed off into the crowd.

Felix gazed at the woman that he admired so much, who filled his evenings with joy. Was Tynemore right? Should he consider keeping her?

It sounded so wrong. But...

The idea hit him hard. What did that mean exactly? How could he keep her?

He could ask her to marry him. It would be a practical arrangement for them both, possibly the best arrangement of all sorts. She did not wish to have a passionate relationship in which she gave herself over to it entirely. She had her own dreams and goals.

He only needed one heir and a spare. They could hire a vast army to raise the children, and he could continue on in his work, and she would always be in his life. It was actually a very good idea.

In fact, it was an excellent idea.

In that moment, he considered going over to Tynemore, shaking his hand, and thanking him for solving his problems.

He would be able to have an intelligent, beautiful woman be his countess. It would be far better than having to go through the fields of young ladies on the marriage mart.

That sounded arrogant, but the fact was that many of the young ladies of the *ton* were not well-read and had no talent except for carrying on their family connections.

He didn't like it, but there it was. It wasn't their fault, of course, but it was a way of society.

And as she came off the dance floor and crossed back to him, she let out a sigh. "I think I need punch."

"Allow me to get you some," he said, his pulse quickening as his idea began to take root.

"Let us go together," she declared. "I wish a moment away from the floor."

And so they went arm-in-arm to the lemonade. He reached forward and took a crystal cup, then handed it to her.

She sipped at it delicately. "This is far more fun than I ever imagined it could be."

"Tynemore has a gift for it," he said. "He makes uncomfortable people comfortable."

"I can see that," she mused. "And he did so with me most immediately."

"What did he say to you?" he queried, uneasy.

"Nothing of much import," she said, growing guarded.

"Oh?" he said, barely able to hold back his curiosity. "You looked…"

Her brows rose. "What?"

"Well, your forehead furrows when you are distressed, and it made me think you were considering something."

"Oh, well…" She grinned and took a deep drink of punch. "I am considering many things. Did you see that they have balloon flights?"

"Would you like to go?" he asked, wondering how the devil he could simply ask her his question.

"Oh, yes!" she exclaimed. "It will be wonderful, and I can write home about it."

She plunked her cup down and all but skipped toward where the beautiful balloons were tied, waiting to take people up into the air.

It was not a new fashion. It had been happening in France and London now for more than twenty years, but it was still thrilling to see. And for Alice it was new, another adventure.

He handed her over into one of the baskets, and he climbed in himself.

"We will not let you go up very far, my lord," said the man organizing the balloons.

"That's quite all right," he said. He didn't want to end up halfway to Paris or Scotland, depending on which way the wind blew.

The man organizing the balloons began to let the weights go until there were just one or two, and the balloon floated upward into the sky. She leaned over, staring out at London beneath them.

They were not terribly high off the ground, but it still gave one a perspective that was far higher than she had likely ever been. He turned and looked at her face, which was full of wonder. He didn't need to look out at London. London was fine. She was the real sight.

He hesitated. "I need to ask you something," he said.

She turned to him, beaming. "What is it?"

"I am in need of a wife, Alice," he stated.

Her smile faded as her gaze searched over his face. "Oh, are you going to start looking for one?"

"I don't think I need to look for one," he said, his voice growing rough.

"You have someone in mind already?" She frowned. "This is an odd thing to say to me. I know that we are friends, but I'm not sure this is appropriate for me to hear—"

"And what if that person was you, Alice?" he blurted. His breath came far more quickly than he liked as his heart began to pound like a horse's hooves at New Market.

"Me?" she exclaimed, staggering back just a bit, causing the basket to sway.

He grabbed hold of her then, carefully. "Yes, I think we should marry. It would be a very good idea."

She tilted her head to the side, her visage perplexed. "How would it be a very good idea?"

He drew in a deep breath, ready to make his argument. "You're business-minded, and you're practical. You know what you want out of this life. You've already told me your aspirations and what you need, and I will not ask a great deal of you. You can continue as you are. We make a wonderful team. We are good friends, and I will not ever be afraid of losing my heart to you because we have been so clear with each other."

She swallowed before she said, "You will never be afraid of losing your heart with me."

"Correct," he said brightly. "We are the best of friends. Are we not? I adore being with you. You make me feel completely alive. But I think that we have not gone too far.

We haven't been foolish."

"Foolish," she repeated, her face turning into a mask. "You wish to marry me because we have not yet been foolish, and I am practical. I suppose that's because I'm a country girl who ran an apothecary and grows flowers."

He winced. This was not going at all as he expected. It had been impulsive, of course, but when he had run it through his mind on the ground, this had seemed like an ideal opportunity.

"Alice," he assured, feeling a wave of panic, "I admire you. I think you would make a wonderful countess."

"I would make a terrible countess," she pointed out firmly.

"Why?"

"Because I plan on spending all of my time running a perfume shop," she pointed out, her voice pitching up.

"Well, I don't need you to do many things," he explained. "I can do a great deal, and you will enjoy having the opportunity of being with people like the Duke of Tynemore, which will allow you to promote your perfumes."

"And children?" she said, her voice dropping as if afraid to ask.

"Well, I need children because of the earldom. We can arrange your schedule so that it's possible and not too taxing for you. I can hire a nanny, several nursemaids, and—"

"Stop!" she said sharply, hard as a slap.

"What?" He managed the word but could not formulate anything else. Indeed, he couldn't think at the intensity of her reply.

"Can you not hear yourself?"

"I hear myself very well," he replied, his blood icing at her tone.

"What you suggest is so horribly cold."

"It is not cold, Alice," he stated. "It is the way of the *ton*.

Even if you were not to have a perfume shop, most ladies do not interact with their children very much. That is why there is a large nursery. And that way, they can go about to balls and events and help their husbands and—"

"Stop, *please*," she cried out, lifting her hands. "You are asking me to marry you, but you wish to have no affection for me. Or our children, it seems."

"Of course I have affection for you, Alice. You're my friend."

"No," she ground out. "Do you not understand that I have come to..." Her voice died off, and a look of horror transformed her face.

"What?" he pressed, longing to reach for her, but his hands felt so leaden. "You've come to what?"

She shook her head and looked away, staring out at the horizon.

"I have been a fool," she said to the night. "A terrible, terrible fool. You understand?"

"No," he rasped. "I don't understand."

"I have been falling for you for weeks. No," she lamented. "That is a lie. I fell for you when we tumbled together in the lavender field. I don't know how it's possible, but in that moment, I knew that I was to love you, and now, I do love you." She stilled, then drew herself up, as if she was donning armor. "But I can tell you this...I will never marry you."

"Alice, please—" he tried to reason, each of her statements a gutting blow.

She would not hear it. "With what you just said to me, how you just said it? You have been alone all your life, and you like it that way, and you want to keep it that way. You want to keep any sort of connection away so you won't get hurt."

"That's not why."

"Yes, it is," she returned, her eyes flashing with pain.

"You think you're protecting everyone, but you are protecting yourself, and that's the truth. I could never accept such a marriage proposal. I thought all this time that I didn't want my mother's life, but I admire her, the love she had with my father. It was cut short too soon, and she loves her children. They give her joy. Yes, she's tired. Yes, it's hard, but..." She looked away. "Take me down. I want off this thing. There has to be a way to take me down."

Dismayed, he tugged on the rope, and immediately the man below began guiding the balloon back down. She climbed out so fast, she almost fell to the ground. He tried to help her up, but she pushed him away.

"Do not ever ask me that again," she said. "I think..." She let out a ragged breath. "This is over. This adventure? It is done. I don't wish to go on like this. It is a ruse that I no longer want a part of."

"A ruse?" he echoed, hardly able to understand how all that they had was unraveling. Instead of keeping her, he was losing her... No, he had already lost her. That's what she was saying.

"I cannot pretend like you can," she proclaimed. She winced and raised a hand to her chest as if her heart was causing her physical pain. "How could you say all of those things? How could you offer me such an empty life without any affection, knowing..."

He shook his head, confused. "Knowing what?"

At his expression, her anger faded, replaced only by resignation. "It does not matter. Thank you for all that you've done. I shall always be grateful, so very grateful, Felix, but I cannot ever accept the life that you have just offered me."

Tears glistened in her eyes as she stepped away from him. They slipped down her cheeks before she ran through the crowd.

He watched her go, his boots frozen to the spot.

In that instant, he knew that he had made the greatest mistake of his life. He never should have asked her to marry him, and he never should have suggested any sort of relationship.

It would've been better if they just kept going as they were, but that was over now.

Over forever. And he had no idea how he was going to survive it.

Chapter Twenty-Six

"Let me in," she begged, banging on the shop door in the night, long after it had closed.

The beautiful glass front rattled. She stood, hoping beyond hope that Madam Clémence would come to the door, that anyone would come to the door and let her in. She certainly did not wish to go back to the townhouse. She could not bear it. That place that had been so happy for her now represented an empty existence in which no hope, no promise, and no possibility dwelt.

She had not realized that she was dwelling in the possibility of a future with him, but that's exactly what she had been doing. And it wasn't the cold sort of future that he imagined for them, in which they went about life as business partners. She did not want to be his business partner. She wanted to be the greatest love of his life. It was ridiculous and absurd and perverse of her.

How she longed to kick herself, to rail at how she could not have seen this coming. But she had not. And torturing herself over her failures surely would not help.

Even so, it was tempting to curse herself for being so naive.

Tears slipped down her face as rain began to fall, and soon she could not tell the difference between the tears on her face and the rain coming down from the sky. She stood in her silk gown, which was now plastered to her body. Her hair tumbled about her face, slicking to her cheeks, and much to her heartbreak, she was forced to pluck the butterflies from her hair, one by one.

Somehow that act felt like the final blow, the death of her hopes.

She leaned against the door and let out a sob. Perhaps she should simply sit upon the pavement and give up, though that was not her usual style. But her usual fortitude seemed to have abandoned her.

Just as she was about to give up, the door swung open.

"You look like a drowned rat, mon chérie." Madam Clémence stood there in her dressing gown, eyes wide, mouth pursed. "I was going to shoot whoever was attempting to break in," she said, holding a pistol by her side, "but I realized it was you, and I think it best I let you in."

Alice stumbled forward into the shop. "Thank you," she said shakily. "Thank you."

Madam Clémence shut the door behind her. "You're lucky I live above the shop and I am here. I have enough money that I do not need to rent a sad little room somewhere."

She shivered as she stood in an ever-growing puddle and her gown dripped water onto the floor. "I thought perhaps you would be like my mother and never want to be away from your things."

"Well, I am not like your mother, my dear. I don't have children; I never have. My work is my family. But I will say that in that regard, yes, I am like your mother." Madame Clémence placed the pistol behind the counter, returning it to a locked drawer, then whipped out a linen sheet from a pile in a cupboard to the left. "I do not wish to go away from my work. I love it here. And you love it, too, but not this much, I think."

She wasn't certain. She thought she loved perfume enough to give up everything. To make it her sole purpose. But in one night she had realized how much she actually admired her mother's life. Even with her disappointments, at least her mother knew love and how to give it. She was a triumphant woman who made her children feel safe, cared for, and beloved.

Madame Clémence thrust the linen at her. "Dry yourself and come along."

Alice did as instructed.

Madam Clémence guided her to the back part of the shop and then up the stairs to where she lived.

She studied the upstairs with growing appreciation.

It was the coziest set of rooms. There was a fire crackling in a small but adequate hearth. A beautiful woven blue-and-red rug covered the floor.

Books were upon every surface and lined a wall of shelves. There were tables with beautiful, embroidered cloths.

And cozy chairs awaited before the fire.

There was a black tea kettle steaming away over the fire, so that Madam Clémence could have a cup of tea whenever she wished, and a marmalade cat sat on the soft blue ottoman right before the fire, warming himself, belly up and paws curved inward.

Clearly he was a happy, happy fellow, which for some reason caused tears to spring to Alice's eyes again. She was never going to be as happy as that bloody cat.

Madame Clémence tsked. "Oh, now, my dear, you are a watering pot all over again."

Shaking her head and asking some more, Clémence

whipped out a handkerchief and gave it to her. "Take care of that business upon your face, my dear. I shall get you something to change into. You cannot stand in that. You will catch your death."

Madame Clémence hurried into another room and came back with an elaborate banyan that was quite long and beautifully embroidered.

"I don't want to take your things," Alice protested, feeling terribly embarrassed that she had nowhere else to go and no one else to turn to.

"Oh, never you fear, I have more than one," Madame Clémence said proudly. "And this is for a good cause. I can see that your heart has been broken. What better thing for my banyan to do than to grace the shoulders of a brokenhearted young woman and give her comfort?"

Pushing it into Alice's hands, she gestured to the sapphire screen panels embroidered with roses in the corner of the room near the fire. "Now go behind that and put the robe on. You'll feel much better."

There was no brooking Madame Clémence, so she did as instructed. She headed behind the screen and slipped off her clothes, which was no easy feat given that they were wet. The buttons were very small, and she managed to tear one of them as she worked the garment off. It was deeply unpleasant, peeling off the gown that had given her so much pleasure just hours before.

With a resigned but grateful sigh, she pulled the banyan on. It was a thick, luscious affair that wrapped her up entirely in beautiful fabric. She came around the screen and tried to smile at her mentor.

"Ah, you still look like a rat, but not quite a drowned one," Clémence observed.

"Thank you for the confidence," Alice teased, though she could not hear any playfulness in her tone.

"My dear, you look most dejected." Clémence gestured to the soft, inviting chair. "Sit."

"I am dejected," she admitted before she came forward and threw herself into the cushioned chair before the fire.

"Tell me all about it," Clémence urged as she took the chair opposite Alice. She sat like a queen, ready to hold court. "It is the earl. He has acted a fool."

"He has acted a fool," she affirmed, her voice shaking.

Clémence snorted. "But of course. He has cast you out, is that it? He has decided no longer to be your amour?"

"He asked me to marry him," she revealed, the horror of it still fresh.

Madame Clémence's eyes bulged, and her hands, which were working over a teapot on the table beside her chair, now stilled. "He asked you to marry him and you were standing outside my shop crying, begging to come in?"

Alice worried her lower lip for a moment. "When you put it like that, it sounds absurd."

"It *is* absurd, my dear," Clémence replied as she spooned tea leaves into the pot painted with blue peonies.

"No, it is not. You should have heard what he said." She couldn't bring herself to relive those awful moments where he'd made love seem so...unpleasant. So unacceptable.

"What did he say, that you're chopped liver?" Madame blew out a sigh. "Paté is marvelous, you know."

"He did not say that I am chopped liver," she returned, now feeling quite confused about the whole evening. After all, her life had been upended. "He said... Well, he said that we would go about life without having any real affection for each other and that way we could essentially be safe. I could run my business, he could be an earl, we'd have children, but that would be the end of it, and we would hire an army of servants to take care of the children so that I did not have to. But he made it sound as if we would all live apart from each other, and I don't know why he would want to marry me if that's what he wanted to do."

"The English aristocracy, my dear," Madam Clémence said with great annoyance, "are very strange fish, very cold. It's from all that sending away, you know."

"Sending away?" she queried, tugging the banyan tighter about herself.

"When they are small, the aristocrats, they are sent away to boarding school or to stay with other families." As she spoke, Madame Clémence poured hot water into the teapot and let it steep. "They do not develop close attachments to their parents unless they're very unusual. There are a few families in England that are very close, that do not send their children away or keep them with nannies and nursemaids, but most children, my dear, here, of the class that Felix is a part of? They only spend thirty to forty-five minutes a day with their children, sometimes not at all because they travel or leave them in the country."

Alice winced. "That sounds terrible."

Clémence nodded as she strained the tea into cups. "I'm assuming you spent every day with your mother and your siblings, and your father when he was alive."

"I did. We were in each other's pockets all of the time," she admitted.

"You see, he knows nothing of this. He does not understand that it could be normal. In fact, it probably frightens him, the idea that he might be able to open up and let someone like you in all of the time."

"But it's wonderful," Alice enthused, thinking of what a mad but wonderful childhood she'd had, and how she knew that if there was anything amiss, her mother or at least one sibling would comfort her.

Madam Clémence tilted her head to the side. "Do you truly think so? Why does he think that you would want to marry him as a business partner?"

She sighed. "Because I told him that I had no wish to be like my mama. I did not want to have a brood of children. I did not want to be stuck behind the counter of her shop with no other options in life."

Madame handed Alice a cup, then went about stirring her own with a silver spoon. "I see, so he was trying to give you what you wished. How very terrible of him."

Alice scowled, flustered by the repositioning of her assumptions. "When you put it like that—"

"I keep putting things in ways you don't like, but there are two ways."

"Still." Alice began savoring the warmth of the tea as she took her first sip. "I have realized… I have realized that I don't want a life without love. My mother was not entirely wrong. She chose my father, and I thought all these years that she regretted giving up her dreams. But now I'm not so certain. I think she's only tired because she just doesn't sleep enough, not because she is weary of her circumstances. She loved the shop, and she loved us. Have I made a terrible mistake?"

Madame sighed. "No, my dear, you have not made a terrible mistake because one must go out into this life and learn. One must have experiences to know what they truly want. Do you wish to be like me, a perfumer who has no family, who has nothing to look forward to except for work until her old age? The truth is my family has all died. I had to leave France after most of them were caught and killed in The Terror. I don't know if I could ever open my heart again to the risk of such pain, and it sounds as if your earl is like that."

"That is exactly what he's like," she groaned. "He seems so afraid of pain, of letting anyone in, of connection."

Madam Clémence nodded. "He may secretly long for it in his heart, but he may never be able to give it to you. So you must not count on it. I am sorry that you have realized that what you want is in many ways what your mother had, and now it's too late. The work will sustain you if he will not realize what the fool he is."

Alice nodded soberly, looking down into her cup of tea.

"I am a fool, too, in my own way," Clémence said jovially, "but I am not miserable. I have a good life, and I have friends like you."

"You think of me as a friend, Madame?" she piped, surprised.

Madame Clémence's face softened. "Oh, oui, of course, you are a boon in my life and I'm so glad that you are part of it."

They sat in silence for a moment, then Madame Clémence ventured, "Perhaps you should come and work for me in the shop front."

"I don't think I would be very good in the shop," she pointed out, "but I will try, and I can't stay with him anymore."

"No, you can't," Clémence agreed, frowning. "Not if you want a different life, not if you are not prepared to give him what he wants."

"I can't," she lamented. "It will destroy me. I cannot live like that, offering my heart up fully, having it crushed and turned away, unwanted whilst he can go through life like an unfeeling statue. I did not know he could be like that. He seemed so kind, so warm."

Madame Clémence opened a box next to her, then pushed it toward Alice. "Take one. Chocolate will do you good. It's excellent for shock and heartbreak."

She peered at the beautifully made treats, hardly daring to pick one but knowing she'd offend Clémence if she did not.

She picked a dark one and nibbled it carefully. The bittersweet notes burst in her mouth, and for a moment she did feel better.

Madame Clémence took one of her own and took a bite. She chewed and considered. "I'm sure he's kind and he is warm, but he is also afraid."

Alice did not know if it was the chocolate, but suddenly she felt emboldened. "May I have my things brought here? Could I stay with you?"

Madame Clémence's eyes widened. "Stay with me, mon chérie. I do not think… Well," Madam Clémence relented, "I do have an extra room. And for a short period of time, perhaps we can get on with each other without killing one another."

Alice arched a brow. "Why would we do that, Madame Clémence?"

"I have lived alone so long, my dear, I do not know how to get on with other people." She set her teacup aside and gave her a gentle smile. "But for you, I will make an exception."

"Thank you," she said, and then tears began to fill her eyes and fall from her cheeks again.

"Oh no," Madam Clémence protested. "A broken-hearted lover in my midst. I do not know how I shall cope. Myself and Marcel here, we shall try to cheer you up."

And with that, Clémence went over to the cat and scratched his tummy.

Marcel woke, jumped down to the ground, and contemplated Alice. The cat stretched, then let out a meow, and much to her surprise jumped onto her lap.

Marcel circled around, plopped himself down, and began purring.

"Ah, a good sign. You are meant to be here until everything sorts itself out."

"But Madame," Alice said softly, "nothing will sort out. Nothing will ever sort itself out again."

She was sure of it.

Chapter Twenty-Seven

Felix knew even before Stevens told him.

The door to the townhouse opened without him having to lift a finger, and somehow that made his whole body ache. He'd forever think of her now in such moments.

He stepped into the townhouse and looked at the grim-faced butler. "Is she gone?"

Stevens nodded. "Yes, my lord. She had all her things taken, and there is a note for you."

He could not bear it. How could she leave? He had been certain that he'd made the right decision. It had seemed like the perfect plan. He'd been so good at plans. Perhaps he'd made a few mistakes, but she'd helped him with those. Certainly now, if he had made mistakes, she could help him again, but it seemed she wanted no part in mending that.

He headed to the table where the note waited. He opened it, his heart pounding, hoping for something profound. For anything. For a reversal in decisions...

The note said none of those things.

All that was scrawled across the white card was a simple

"thank you."

That was all.

She had cut him from her life with a simple "thank you," all because... Dear God, he could not keep playing it through his mind.

She loved him.

She had fallen in love with him. He had spent all his life trying to prevent this from happening, and now it had.

He crumpled the note in his hand, whipped round, and stormed out the door. There was really only one thing to do. He was going to have to go to the club. He was going to have to get dead drunk.

Felix stormed down to his coach, climbed in, banged on the roof, and called out the destination. They rumbled through the dark night, and he ground his teeth. This had been the greatest mistake of his life.

Bloody hell, what had he been thinking? He should have just let things stay as they were. They had been happy. And then he'd had to push, try for more happiness. It was ridiculous.

And as the coach pulled up in front of his club, he stomped down, headed inside, and called for brandy. The porters and butlers stared at him as he pounded up and found a fairly empty room.

The few fellows playing billiards took one look at him and headed out.

The butler on duty brought him a glass.

"I don't want a glass," he said. "I want the bottle."

The butler inclined his head and left the decanter beside him.

"Thank you," he called, unable to embrace rudeness fully. Felix poured out a glass and started to drink.

"You know, you can't do that alone," a familiar voice said.

Felix glanced back over his shoulder. "What the devil are you talking about?"

"Drinking alone?" Tynemore drawled. "It's disastrous for one's health. Ask me and I shall tell you how I know."

He swung his gaze back to his friend, gripping the crystal snifter in his hand. "I think you've done enough."

"I don't think I have," Tynemore disagreed. "As a matter of fact, I'm fairly certain I haven't even begun."

"Go," Felix ground out. "I don't want anyone here."

"You don't mean that," Tynemore countered.

"I do," he retorted before he sucked in a harsh breath. "I've lost her."

"How?" Tynemore demanded.

He laughed a slow, bitter sound that bounced off the walls and ceiling. "I asked her to marry me."

"Good, I'm glad you asked her to marry her. What did she say?"

Felix let out a snort and tossed back the contents of the brandy. "Clearly she did not say yes."

"Well, it doesn't seem like it, but I didn't want to assume," Tynemore said, crossing the room. "Pour me a glass."

"I don't want to drink with you. You've cocked everything up."

"I have?" Tynemore said, his brows rising. "My goodness, I had no idea you were so capable of playing the victim."

"I? Play the victim?" Felix growled. He poured out another glass but did not pour one for his friend. He tossed the contents back. "She has left me. She has even taken everything from the townhouse."

"Bloody hell, old boy, she must be sending you a very strong message."

"A message?" he echoed.

"Yes." A muscle tightened in Tynemore's jaw. "She didn't like what you said. What *did* you say?"

He stared at the contents of his brandy, willing some sort of explanation to be at the bottom of the amber liquid, but none arose. "I asked her to marry me. I was going to give her everything that she wanted."

"And what exactly do you think that she wants?" Tynemore asked, putting his hands down on the table, staring at his friend.

He shrugged. "I thought she wanted independence. She wants to run a shop. She doesn't want to be tied down by family or love. I thought we were perfect for each other."

Tynemore rolled his eyes. "In many ways, the two of you are perfect for each other in your delusions."

"Delusions?" he challenged, gripping the snifter so hard he felt the cut crystal press into his palm.

"The idea that you two don't want love?" Tynemore blew out a derisive sound. "It's ridiculous, and I'm not hearing any more about it."

"But that is exactly what I want," Felix insisted, beginning to feel the brandy burn through his system.

"Well, it's clearly not what she wants, is it?" Tynemore drawled.

Felix tossed the brandy back again.

"Slow down. You're going to regret it. You're going to feel like death tomorrow. And then when you go and you try to get her—"

"I'm not going to try and get her," Felix said flatly. "I'm going to let her go."

"Why in God's name would you do that?"

"Because she doesn't want me, not the way I am. And she wants something I cannot give her." The words grated his throat. "So why would I do that to her?"

"Why can't you give it to her?" Tynemore demanded, his gaze hardening with impatience.

"You know why," Felix snapped.

"I don't," Tynemore said, unyielding now as he leaned forward, hands braced on the table. "You've built up this imaginary wall to protect your heart and your head, and none of it works. Look at you. You're standing here swilling brandy to stop the pain."

"I'm not in pain," he ground out.

"You're not in pain?" Tynemore threw back his head and laughed. "If anyone knows pain, I do. You're losing her."

"I've already lost her," he countered.

Tynemore stilled then and said quietly, "No, there's still a chance."

"Either you leave, or I leave," he stated, unable to bear this conversation any longer.

Tynemore eyed his friend. "I am sorry for you," he said at last, "if this is all you're willing to do, if this is how little you esteem her."

"What the bloody hell do you mean by that?" Felix roared.

Tynemore blinked, hesitating, as if considering whether he should go on. But then the duke drew in a long breath and began, "I lost my wife. She died. I would give anything for a few moments with her again, to tell her that I love her, to tell her how much I care, how she changed my world, how she made it better. I wouldn't throw it away. But look at you. You have the greatest opportunity at love, at life, at a family, and you are throwing it in the bin."

"This is not the same as—"

Tynemore pulled back and shook his head. "You don't deserve her."

"I never said I did," he hissed, even as it felt as if his heart was cracking.

"Good God, man," Tynemore realized as his gaze widened with understanding. "You just can't bear it, can you?"

"What?" he growled, wishing to God that his friend would just leave him. That the pain of it all could just stop.

"That someone might love you, that you might love someone in turn, that you might be willing to take a risk."

Risk. He thought of all the times that he had dared her to adventure.

Tynemore shook his head with dismay. "It pains me to say it, but I must. You're being a coward, my friend."

Coward. Perhaps he was.

He swallowed. It was as if Tynemore was saying exactly what he thought in his head. He'd dared her to adventure so many times, and she had taken him up on the challenge, but he could not, dared not go down that road. He'd promised himself, and he did not break promises. He could not afford to learn to soften.

He turned away from his friend, and his shoulders sagged. "I don't know what to do," he said. "I have grown so accustomed to her in my life. She makes everything better."

"Go and get her, then."

"I can't," he said. "She doesn't want me."

"She *loves* you," Tynemore said.

"She *thinks* that she loves me," he countered. "She loves a man that in her mind can give her everything, can give it all. But I can't do that."

"Only you can know what you can give and what you can't," Tynemore said, closing the distance between them. He grabbed his shoulder. "But if you let this go, you will regret it for the rest of your life. And I promise you this…"

"What?" he bit out.

Tynemore's eyes grew dark with memory and the knowledge of suffering. "No matter what you choose, there is the chance of pain. But I know this: if you let her go now, you will suffer for the rest of your life. If you choose her, perhaps one day, one of you will suffer, but you will have years of glory, years of love. Don't miss that chance, my friend."

And with that, Tynemore took the bottle of Brandy, poured himself a glass, then tossed it back. He then slammed the glass down and started for the door.

"What the devil are you doing?" Felix called.

"You want to be alone." Tynemore paused and glanced over his shoulder. "And that's the problem. You think that being alone will solve everything." He let out a dry laugh. "Felix, you won't even let *me* be alone. You keep checking on me, making sure I'm all right. You know I'm not all right, but look at you. You are no better. You are worse. My wife was taken from me. But you choose to be alone on purpose. And so, I will give you your wish, just as Alice has done. And I pray you come to your senses. I will always be there for you. I'm your friend, just as you have always been there for me. Wake up, man. Wake the bloody hell up."

Tynemore strode out of the room without another word.

Felix picked up the glass, stared at it, then threw it across the room. It shattered against the wall, and then he cursed himself. He'd have to clean it up. He wouldn't leave his messes for other people to clean. But surely, he had done that already. He had created a mess, and he did not even know how to sort this out.

He wasn't sure he ever could.

Chapter Twenty-Eight

Every day was an agony, and every hour she spent in the shop at the front, helping customers, was an eternity.

She did not know how the attendants did it, but now she understood why the young woman Joanne, who had first greeted her and was rude, was so important. She'd always thought it was a mistake not to let such people go, but now she understood Clémence's reasoning.

Customers were the very devil.

She had no wish to interact with these sorts of people. They were nothing like the guests at Lord Tynemore's house. These were picky, difficult, challenging people who were never pleased. And when they were pleased, sometimes they did not pay their bill for a full year.

She had realized that there was one particular person who owed Madame Clémence over two hundred pounds. Clémence was kind and had not yet set the bailiffs on the person.

There was also a duke—not the Duke of Tynemore, for he was honest and good—who owed her the same sum but did not pay because his reputation was so vast and important that merely having the association brought customers to her.

It was an absurd state of affairs, but there it was.

She ground her teeth as a dandy of a lord started toward her.

Madame Clémence gave her a strange look and called to her. "Come, Alice. You must come back."

Relieved, she pulled off her frilly apron and headed into the back with Madame Clémence, who took her into the room where she'd first begun sorting herbs. It had been quite some time since that first day, and she had learned so much from Madame in the art of perfume making. She felt quite confident now, but she was not confident in being able to run a shop, not like this.

Clémence let out a beleaguered sigh. "I cannot have your sour face around the customers, my dear. I am so sorry. I adore you, but at present, it is not a good idea. With your love gone—"

"I don't think it's about him," she snapped, as her heart spasmed. And then she wished to kick herself. How could she snap at Clémence, who had been so supportive? "Forgive me, Madame Clémence," she said. "You have been nothing but kind to me, but I do not think the way I feel out there has anything to do with Felix."

Madame Clémence's eyebrow shot up. "I dislike having to tell you this, my dear, but when one makes a cake without sugar, it is not sweet. You are trying to help people find something, find passion, and you have none yourself anymore. This is going to cause you difficulties. You are now a dried-out sponge."

Her mouth dropped open. "Madame Clémence, you cannot say such a thing."

"I can, my dear, because it is true," Clémence countered. "I adore you, but this must be said. You go about life as if you are a sponge that has been wrung out or a lemon that has been squeezed. You must find a solution. It has been weeks."

It had been weeks.

Brutal, awful, heart-rending weeks. He had not come. She did not know why she thought he might, but she had. She had thought perhaps one day he would realize his mistake, that he would come to the shop, get on his knees, beg her forgiveness, and declare his love for her. It was the stuff of novels and fiction, the stuff of plays and operas.

Madame Clémence tsked. "You are still pining after him, and I imagine you will for some time. So I think we shall put you in the back where you can make beautiful perfume. That is where you thrive in any event, my dear. The last one you created, sheer genius! Everyone loves it. I would wear it myself."

And she had noticed that Madame Clémence *did* wear it.

The truth was Madame Clémence's decision filled her with relief, not anger. She hated running the shop.

"I think, my dear," Clémence mused, "your genius is not in the running of the shop, but in the supplying of perfumes. Do you want to have your own establishment, or would you be happier supplying my establishment? I will gladly set you up, so that you can be independent and make all the perfumes you desire."

She blinked. "I don't even know if I like London anymore," she said, her heart sinking.

"Ah, you miss home," Madame Clémence said. "I understand. I still miss France."

She shook her head. "How do I explain? I miss the comfort of it. Being safe there."

"People do not grow when they're safe," Clémence said. "You have grown so much here."

She nodded, but nor did she wish to discuss the depths of her feelings any more. "The back will do very well," she said.

"I do like making the perfumes, and I do not like interacting with those lords and ladies. None of them were like that at the duke's."

"None of them are associates with the duke." Madame Clémence waggled her brows. "They wish they were. And if they knew that you had been to his establishment, they would all be green with jealousy and they would be clamoring to leave me and use you. So perhaps you should open your own shop and you should tell everyone that the Duke of Tynemore is your dear friend."

"I can't do that," she said flatly.

"Why?" Madame Clémence asked, exasperated.

"Because he is the earl's dearest friend," she said with a shrug. "I have left all that behind."

Madame frowned. "You are not a businesswoman at all. You should have married the earl and dealt with his silliness. And perhaps one day he would have come around to you. I think, my dear, that perhaps you should go to him and tell him yes."

"I can't do that," she declared, awash with dismay.

"Why?" Clémence tsked. "Because of your pride?"

"No," she said, lifting her chin. "Because I deserve more. I deserve love. And he deserves it, too. But if he cannot see it, I will not beg."

Madame Clémence nodded. "I suppose I understand, but I will tell you that if I could have my family back, I would not be so proud. I would take any course that I needed to win them all back."

"I understand, Madame," she said. "But this is different. You were taken from them. They were taken from you. He has willfully left me."

"Madame," a voice called. "There is a note for Miss Alice."

The young attendant came forward and offered it to her.

Alice's heart leaped into her throat. She did not usually get communications. She stared at it. It was not the earl's handwriting; it was her mother's. She took the letter and thanked the girl.

She ripped it open and read quickly. Her spirits sank and fear laced through her blood. "Robert, my brother, is very ill. He has been sick for a week. She's asking me to come home. She's afraid he will not survive this."

"Then you must go." Madame Clémence took her hand. "You must go immediately. Take the fastest coach that you can."

"I do not have enough for a ticket—"

"I will give you the money," Clémence said. "Go as swiftly as you can."

She nodded, her heart full at her mentor's generosity. Even so, she could barely think of anything as her brother's condition overtook her.

Still, she managed to get out, "Thank you, Madame Clémence. Thank you."

Not able to wait another moment, she ran to her room upstairs. She gazed at the small chamber that had been her comfort. Marcel meowed and climbed toward her. She petted the cat, scratching his chin, and then picked him up and held him to her chest.

"Oh, Marcel," she lamented. "It's all going terribly wrong. All my dreams are breaking. And my brother…"

The cat meowed again, then head-butted her, stroking his head along her chin, as if somehow that would solve all of her problems. It did not, but at least it alleviated a brief moment of suffering.

The cat began to purr.

She hugged him closer, and then she put him down to pack a small valise. As soon as she clicked the clasps, she did not know if she would ever return to London, to Madame

Clémence, to the earl. She did not know if she would ever see any of this again because her mother needed her. Her family needed her.

She had thought all of this was so important, but now with the crumpled note in her hand, realizing that Robert could be taken at any moment, she thought of what Madame Clémence said, how Madame Clémence desperately wished she could have her family back. Alice had run away from her family, hoping to find happiness here, fulfillment here, but she had not found it. Oh, she had learned new skills, and she was deeply grateful for them, but she was emptier now, more broken, more brittle. She had lost her optimism. She had lost her belief that all would work out. And so, now, as she slipped down the hall, heading out to find Madame Clémence to get the money for a coach, she was terrified.

Terrified that it all would not work out, terrified that Robert could be taken from them, that her life was about to plunge into a very dark chapter indeed. Her love was gone, her family was in jeopardy, and she had no idea what the future might bring.

Madame slipped the coins into her palm. "I have called for a coach to collect you. It is dear in cost, but with your brother so ill, a public coach with many stops will take too long. The coach will take you all the way out to Cornwall. And do not let your mind get the better of you. You are made of very strong stuff indeed. And remember, I am your friend, and I shall always be here for you."

Alice nodded before she wrapped her arms about her mentor.

Madame Clémence let out an exclamation of surprise. She patted Alice's back gently. "Thank you, my dear, thank you."

Not daring to wait another moment, Alice raced out into the streets to leave London, to leave the place that she had always dreamed of coming, to leave the place where she thought her dreams would be made.

And instead, she went home, praying, praying she would find a way to mend her broken heart and that fate would not take everything from her for having the audacity to want too much.

Chapter Twenty-Nine

"You look like hell."

Felix was in no mood to hear Tynemore's commentary about his life, especially after their last run-in. He loved his friend, he cared about him, but he did not want to be anywhere near him and his sermonizing right now, nor his superiority or the fact that he was proving right.

Because the fact was, Felix felt like hell.

"I thought you were going to leave me alone as I wished," he rumbled.

Tynemore snorted. "Well, I planned on it, but your butler came to me in quite a state."

"What?" he demanded, his jaw clenching, and he ground out, "He has no business."

Tynemore ventured into the dark room. "Apparently, you have not been reading your reports or your mail, and you've been staying in your room except for when you go out to work. He's quite concerned about you and decided the only thing for it was to come to me."

"I'm going to Horse Guards. I'm doing what's required of

me," he defended.

"No, this is not about Horse Guards," Tynemore cut in. "These are reports from Bow Street."

"Bow Street?" he gasped, his blood chilling.

"Good God, man, how long have you been sitting here in the dark?" Tynemore crossed to the windows and threw open the curtains. "I know grief, and I know self-pity, and you are definitely reveling in it."

"I don't have anything to grieve. I have not suffered like you," he stated.

Tynemore folded his arms across his chest, clearly ready to do battle. "No, you haven't. I agree with you, but you are grieving because you've lost something, haven't you? And now it hurts."

It did hurt. It hurt more than anything he'd ever known. He had not known he had the capacity for this kind of pain. He had suffered all his life in various ways. He'd been lonely, but this was new. He felt as if he'd had a limb severed from his body. Only this was actually far worse. It wasn't his limb. It was his soul. He felt empty, hollow, adrift without purpose.

How had he lived without her before they met, and how was he going to live without her now that he'd lost her?

She'd made it clear she did not wish to see him again. Surely, he should respect that, but this was a new piece. "What does Bow Street say?" he demanded.

His friend arched a brow. "You assume I've read the reports?"

He rolled his eyes. "Of course you have."

Tynemore nodded before he leveled, "They've captured Bilby."

"Where?" he demanded, his breath hitching with alarm. Had the man been so close? He'd assumed Bilby had run to the Continent to try to save his neck.

"Just outside Helexton." Tynemore's eyes narrowed.

"Apparently, the man was lurking about the estate. He was drunk, frustrated, and armed. The magistrates have already taken him. He's been sentenced, and he's to be deported to Australia."

"Thank God," he breathed. "He can't hurt Alice or her family."

But he did not feel much relief or solace. As a matter of fact, if he had been in hell just a moment before, now he descended to the very pits.

He wiped a hand over his face. "My God, what am I doing?"

"I don't know, but whatever it is, you need to stop," Tynemore agreed.

"I'm being so selfish," he said.

"Yes, you are." His friend crouched down before him.

"If I had not appointed those Bow Street runners, her family, she…" He swallowed, thinking of how badly things might have gone. "Alice, is she all right? Did Bilby follow her here at all?"

"She's not even in London," Tynemore informed gently.

A stone dropped in his gut. "What?"

"She's gone to Cornwall." Tynemore let out a sigh of impatience. "Did you not read any of the notes that were sent to you?"

"I have avoided anything but work," he admitted, rankling at the well-deserved censure.

Tynemore blew out a breath. "You are going to be the ruin of yourself, you know? Madame Clémence sent a note. She wanted you to know Alice has gone to Cornwall."

"Yes, but clearly, she doesn't want me to know," he pointed out. "She didn't send it herself."

Tynemore paused, then said quietly, "Her brother Robert is sick. She had to leave quickly."

"Robert?" Alarm crashed through him. He thought of

the bright boy who was learning Homer and who dreamed of studying at Oxford.

"Yes, apparently he is not doing well at all. There's fear he might not make it."

Without another thought, Felix pushed himself to his feet. He'd been on the floor too long, though, and he staggered. He had not bathed, and he had not slept well. He had paced the floor at night, unable to stop thinking about her, unable to stop thinking about the way he had hurt her and let her down, and how he did not know how to reach out to her.

A life alone had not prepared him for this. What was worse was he had realized in all his pacing that in all actuality, he desperately wanted to belong to something, but he didn't know how.

He was certain he would wreck it, ruin it. He didn't even know how to ask to get it.

Tynemore crossed to him, clapped his hand on his shoulder, and said, "You need to shake yourself out of this and realize that you deserve love. Your parents were taken from you, but that was not your fault."

"This is not about my parents," he bit out.

But the look that Tynemore gave him was unyielding. It cracked his resistance, and the sting of it was so intense he could not draw breath.

"It f-felt like it was my fault," he admitted at long last, the words torture in his throat. "I felt like I was being punished for something that I did wrong. I don't know what it was."

"You were a child," Tynemore said gently. "So, of course, you told yourself that it was your fault. Children have the strangest minds. They're always certain it's their fault," he added, "but it is not your fault that you are alone, and you don't have to be alone any longer. She wants you. She's waiting for you."

"No, she's not," he cut in. "She left, and for good reason. I offered her… God, when I think of what I offered her."

"Well, it wasn't so very terrible," Tynemore defended. "You offered her security. You offered her a future, and actually you offered her dreams. But do you see, she realized that her dream wasn't exactly what she wanted, and you can do the same, my friend. You can realize that all those vows and promises you made? They can change. You do not have to be who you always were. What is this life, if you aren't going to grow?"

He locked gazes with his friend. "How the devil did you become so wise?"

"Suffering," Tynemore replied honestly. "It's damned annoying but true. You see, this life? It is meant for us to grow in, and she will help you grow. Don't you dare let her go. If you do, I don't know if I'll ever be able to look upon you again."

"I don't know if I'll ever be able to look upon me again, either," he concurred.

The truth was he had been avoiding mirrors these last days, disgusted with himself, but it hurt so much. The pain inside him was so vast. This thing he felt he had to cross to earn love, to have it? It seemed an ocean.

He'd told himself for so long that he simply could not bear to pass the pain of death to others. He'd seen all the people that he'd had to inform of loss during this bloody, long war.

But it was far deeper than that and went back far, far beyond the war. It went back to a little boy who was waiting for his mother and father to come home, but whose mother and father never did.

He could remember, dear God, the howling suffering of it, of being cut adrift with no one to love him, only servants to care for him. He had convinced himself that it had meant nothing, that his parents had spent little time with him, so he was fine. But it had been a lie because he could still remember his mother's face as she leaned over his bed and sang to him every night before she went out. He could still remember his father's strong shoulders as he hoisted him up on them and carried him out for long walks over the fields and through Hyde Park when they were in town.

He had tried to protect himself from the memories of having his family ripped away, tried to protect himself so fiercely that he did not want a family again. Thus, he would not have to go through that again. But now, the pain of being alone far outweighed the pain of risking love.

He had only learned that by throwing it away. Could he try again?

Most never got a second chance. Would he be one of the lucky few?

"Go to her," Tynemore insisted. "Do not leave her alone, and do not let her go through this trouble by herself. She will need you. Her family will need you, if her brother is ill."

He nodded. "I will go no matter the outcome. No matter, if she tells me no. I will not leave her to suffer alone."

Not as he had done all these years. It was time to change. And to grow. And hopefully that would include love, if she would but have him.

Chapter Thirty

Robert was going to live.

It had been touch-and-go for several days. Alice could hardly believe that he had rallied through. The nights had been terrible. She would not be able to shake the horror of his coughing, the way his chest shook as he struggled to draw breath through the night, for some time. If ever.

They had used every herb they could, every salve. They had boiled tea kettles, filling the room with warm steam, and they had prayed.

Dear God, how they had prayed to anyone who would listen. They had called upon her father. They had called upon God. They had called upon the heavens to save him, and one morning his fever broke and he woke and he was able to draw a breath. He still coughed and he still looked quite fragile, but he could sit up now before the beautiful tall windows in the library and read the books that he so adored.

Helexton was still her family's temporary home. They were happy there. She could not believe that she was living in the beautiful building that had given her so much pleasure in the past, but the earl had never asked his mother to leave, and Mrs. Brooke had been quite firm that the family should stay. After all, it would take some time for the shop to be rebuilt.

Her brothers and sisters were so happy at Helexton. One day they would have to leave. One day, hopefully with all her funds from creating perfumes, she could build them a beautiful new shop and home.

But for now, despite what had happened, she was grateful Felix allowed her family to stay at Helexton, giving them a sense of security and continuity.

Her siblings played up and down the long halls and ran outside. Their spirits were wild now, free, full of promise. And the library! Goodness, her brother reveled in it. He read almost a book a day, and her mother thrived in the gardens, tending to the plants and flowers there, making them grow anew.

She spent hours planning with the head gardener who had only just been hired. They pored over books, deciding what best to grow to create a garden that would thrive.

Alice hated the fact that eventually they would have to leave. After all, this was Felix's home, and one day he might return to it to live there. He would not want her there. He would not want a reminder of them. Perhaps, because of her, he would never return. He would not wish to be reminded of that night in a hot air balloon and how she had turned him down, casting his offer aside.

Her heart ached as she strode through the lavender fields. She skimmed her fingers over the petals. She wanted to feel at one with him, even though she would never see him. It was the cruelest thing she could do to herself, and yet she could not stop herself from wandering along the plants, drinking in their heady scent, and wishing she could go back and change things.

She could not, but she could relive that happy moment

when they had met, over and over, couldn't she? She could draw comfort from the fact that she had loved him for a short while.

Who was she fooling? She would love him forever. He would be like a plaintive melody that played through her mind and heart for the rest of her life, just out of reach, always there but never fully hers.

She swallowed and blinked back tears. She brought her hands to her eyes.

"Tears cannot be good for lavender," a man said. A man who sounded like Felix. "I beg you to please stop. The owner of these fields will not allow any harm to the plants."

She tensed. Her hands dug into her skirt. Surely, she was imagining things. The last sleepless, fearful days had stolen her wits! That was it. He couldn't be here. He couldn't. Her heart twisted, aching, longing for him but knowing how he truly felt. Slowly, she turned to that voice, half expecting to see empty air.

But there her glorious, handsome earl stood. His visage a riot of emotion.

"You, sir, must get your boots off my lavender," she began, her lips trembling as she tried to tease. Oh, but it hurt, attempting to be playful when all had been lost. "You are trodding upon it."

He wasn't. But she couldn't resist a moment's echo of their first meeting.

He crossed to her slowly through the lavender. "I shall be more careful," he said, "to keep off your lavender. And it is yours…just like—"

"Why are you here?" she asked, so startled to see him she was half certain he would suddenly vanish.

He stopped a few feet before her. "I just came from your mother at the house," he said.

"Is that how you found me?" she queried.

He nodded. "I was very worried about your brother."

"Robert will recover," she said, relieved she could tell him so.

He nodded. "I am grateful to hear it. He's such a dear boy with so much promise."

She shook her head. "How did you know he was ill?"

"Madame Clémence sent me word."

"Madame Clémence," she breathed. "Of course. She seems to think…"

"What?" he prompted, his eyes widening with emotion.

She shook her head. No. She would not allow her mind to play tricks, seeing things in his gaze that surely were not there. "It doesn't matter what anyone thinks. Felix, it is kind that you came to check on my brother, but why are you truly here? Unless you have come to reclaim your house?"

"I have come to reclaim *you*," he said before he crossed the distance between them and took her hands in his.

She started to pull away. "No," she said.

"No?"

"You don't want me, Felix," she proclaimed as tears began to threaten. She blinked fiercely, determined to keep them at bay. She had to be strong. "You don't."

"I am capable of changing," he protested. "As Tynemore has so recently made clear to me. Just as you are."

"What do you mean by that?"

"You wish for more, don't you?" he challenged. "More love, more affection, and now you wish to have a family that you can love."

She bit her lower lip, hardly believing they were discussing this. For it was too painful. Too awful to do again. And yet… What if?

"I wish to have what my mother had, but without the suffering," she admitted.

"Alice, I cannot promise you a life with no suffering," he

began. "I have spent the last few weeks suffering intensely since you left me, but I deserved it and I needed to. As awful as it was, if I hadn't suffered like that, I wouldn't have understood what I was doing, what I had done to you...what I had done to *us*."

"And what did you do?" she queried, her pulse beginning to skip. Not with hope. She did not dare hope, did she?

His gaze darkened, and this time, he reached out and took her hand, lacing his fingers with hers. "I drove you away because I could not bear to lose you."

"That is a strange paradox," she said, savoring the feel of their hands entwined, barely daring to believe he was within her reach again. But also fearing it would all be yanked away again.

"It is indeed, my love," he said gently. "I told you I did not love you." He shook his head. "We were both mistaken. I am an excellent liar. At least in this. You see, I too have loved you since this field. I have loved you since you told me to get my hands off these lavender petals. You crept into my heart in those moments, and you did not let go. I thought that if I called us friends, that if I just made it about being intimate with you and helping you, that I could avoid the truth, but it was always there. You were meant to be mine. You were always meant to be mine, Alice. Just like I was always meant to be yours."

She gasped. "I don't understand. Why have you turned about so quickly?"

"Because I can spend a life suffering without you or I could spend a life loving you. Pain comes to us all, Alice. I know that now. What a fool I was to run and try to avoid it. I cannot do that, and so I want to stop running. I want to live my life with you, however you want it.

"If you want a large family," he said, "we can have a large family. If you wish to have a shop in London, we can do that, too, but what I would love most of all is to stay here at Helexton with you for most of the year. Your family must stay with us and you can plant what you like, fill the halls with dried flowers and herbs. Take it over and fill it with life."

A soft breath escaped her lips as she stared, stunned.

The muscles in his throat worked as he continued, "You have offered me something so wonderful, so big that I scarce believe I deserve it. Can I please be a part of your life? Can you please let me love you? Can you please let me understand what it means to choose love?"

"What about your work?" she asked, her eyes flooding with tears of a very different kind. It was almost impossible to believe that he was here, saying these things. But she could feel his hand about hers, and his gaze was riveting as he proclaimed his love.

"Horse Guards? Because of you, I have learned that it isn't the lack of love that keeps us safe. No, it is love that makes our lives have meaning. And so, no matter what it takes, I will be here with you. Building my life with you. I can go to London only when I must. I can give up the daily madness, the belief that I must be there every instant to make a difference. It's not true. Any difference I can make? It starts with you. It starts with us," he promised, gently tugging her closer.

"You would change all of that for me? Your whole way of life?" She whispered.

He was silent for a moment, holding her gaze, determined that she should understand how seriously he felt about his.

"I would," he said without hesitation. "I *will*. And you," he said, "what about your work? Do you not wish your own store now?"

It was a fair question. "I don't think I actually ever did," she confessed, overwhelmed by his words and her own realizations. "I have found that I do not actually wish to be in London. I like the city very much, and I love Madame Clémence, but my joy is in the creation of perfumes, and I can do that anywhere now that I know how to do it. I can happily send my perfumes to Clémence for her to sell. And…I am proud of what you do at Horse Guards, keeping so many safe. So I can come to London with you, whenever you need to go. We don't need to ever be apart. After all, you have already bought me so many wonderful tools to make my perfumes. With those beautiful gifts of science? I can work anywhere, too."

She gazed up at her towering earl and confessed, "My dream was never to open a shop, I've realized. My dream was to learn how to make perfume an art, and here at Helexton, I could spend my life doing that."

"Then let me offer it to you," he said. "Let this home be our home. Let us make it a haven for all. For hope, for love, for being together. I don't ever want to be alone again, Alice."

"You don't ever have to be alone," she promised, holding her other hand out to him. "I will always be with you if you wish."

"Oh, I wish, Alice. I wish with all my heart."

And with that, he pulled her into his arms, tilted her head back, and kissed her there in the lavender.

Epilogue

Three years later

Alice kissed the top of her little boy's head and drank in his gentle scent. The acres of rose fields stretching out before them could not compete with the beauty of her child, Christopher, who was but two years old.

A smile parted her lips. She could not stop herself. Life was so very good. She'd found love, her child was healthy, her family was secure, and much to her mother's joy, with Felix's help, Robert was thriving at Oxford.

"It's good to see you smile," her mother said, crossing to her with a basket of roses in hand. "After all this time, do you still not regret coming back from London?"

Alice's throat tightened, surprised by the question. After all, so many seasons had passed since she'd chosen Helexton. She hoped she had not let her down by choosing to come home.

Her mother lowered herself to sit on the blanket, stretched out over the sprawling grass that overlooked the rose fields.

On this glorious June day with the sky a soul-lifting azure, a picnic had seemed just the thing.

Felix and her siblings were on the grass, playing, running back and forth, catching balls, laughing, falling to the earth, and making merry.

"I do not regret it for anything in moments like this," she said, savoring the feel of the small, trusting body nestling against her.

"But you do regret it?" her mother said softly, reaching out and touching her grandchild's hand, clasping the small fingers with her wrinkled ones.

She studied her mother's worn face, wanting to speak the truth. For now, all she longed for was happiness. "I don't regret leaving London at all. I don't regret not opening a shop. I used to think, Mama, that you regretted the choices that you made, that you were heartbroken, that you wished your life was different."

"Oh, my dear," her mother said gently, her face creasing. "That's not at all…"

"It's alright, Mama," Alice cut in. "I realized how mistaken I was. You loved each and every one of us, didn't you? You even loved your work in the apothecary. What filled you with regret was the loss of Papa."

Alice's voice hitched in her throat, for she, too, still missed her father. And even the hint of an idea that she could lose Felix through some chance only made her feel the deepest sympathy for her mother.

Her mother moved her hand from Christopher's to cup Alice's cheek. Her eyes filled with tears, even after so many years. "Oh, my dear, yes. I think you understand now, and I wish that I could have explained it to you when you were a girl. I knew how desperately you wanted me to become a perfumer, as if somehow, I had thrown my dreams aside."

The tears faded and a wise smile, full of love, warmed her

face. "The dream that was thrown aside, well, it was my life with your father, and it wasn't truly thrown away. It was *taken* from me, you see. That was why my heart was full of regret, and that was why I sometimes looked so tired and why it was so difficult for me to put foot after foot. It was so hard to do it alone. It was never supposed to be that way.

"The apothecary with him? That was our dream and a family. I had never known more happiness than when I was with him, when we were all together, but when he was taken away, at least I had you children, and I'm glad you see that now: that I did not waste my life or throw my dreams away."

"Oh, Mama," she said, full of emotion, and she leaned forward, hugging her mother tightly in her arms, careful of the small form of her son. He let out a laugh delighted to be so swallowed up in love.

"Now, come," her mother began as she leaned back and held her arms out to Christopher. "Let me walk with my grandson."

She slipped Christopher onto his feet and began walking with him toward the roses, slowly, taking time to point out the various blooms and bring the boy's nose to the petals.

It was perhaps the most vulnerable her mother had ever been with Alice. She leaned back on her palms, her heart almost aching at the sight of her mother introducing her child to their wonderous world.

Just as she was about to close her eyes and turn her face up toward the sun, Felix came striding up, his eyes aglow with love and joy from his interactions with her family. For he belonged now, too. He did not face the wide world alone.

He sat down beside her, then pulled her gently into his arms. "Are you well, my love? Is everything all right with your mother?"

She leaned into his warm embrace, letting herself feel his strength. "Oh, yes," she said. "We were simply talking about our dreams."

He stared down at her, his gaze trailing over her face. "Dreams? Not regrets?"

She smiled up at him. "There are no regrets, Felix. There is only the future and hope. This is the life that I want, here, with you, amidst the flowers and with our child. Our children," she said, touching her middle, for another was on the way. And she was overjoyed.

It had been a striking thing to realize that her mother's joy had not come from the shop and from the perfumes alone, but from the family that she had created.

And that's what Alice wanted for herself: laughter, love, rambunctious energy, and the comfort of warm embraces. Oh, she still had her work. She'd never give it up. Madame Clémence would never forgive her if she did!

No, her work and herb rooms were full to bursting, and she employed several villagers to assist her in the creation of new perfumes to sell in Madame Clémence's shop...a shop that now bore her name, too. They were the perfect partnership.

And she would never have to be afraid that she would be left to face the cruelty of the world without care. She was surrounded now by family and love and Felix.

Oh, Felix. He was the love of her life, and she, his.

His eyes widened as he stared down at her. "What are you thinking?" he asked.

"Only that nothing else could be more beautiful than this, not even a shop in London." She laughed. "Especially not a shop in London. I cannot bear customers."

"But you can bear me?" he teased.

"Bear you?" she said. "You are my joy, my love. It is you who helps me to bear the hard things in life."

"And you and our family are the joy of *my* life," he declared, his voice rough with emotion.

She pulled his head down to hers for a soft kiss. The moment his lips touched hers, she knew that whatever dreams or nightmares came, whatever her heart desired, whatever life brought, he would be there by her side, her partner, friend, her love.

Acknowledgments

A book takes so many wonderful hands to bring it to the reader, but first I want to thank all my lovely readers. Without you, this story would live only in my head. I am grateful it is so shared! What would I do without my absolutely wonderful, generous, and giving editor, Lydia? You make the process a joy. Thank you, Lydia, for all you do and making me the best I can be. Thank you to Jessica and Liz for always believing in me and making me feel part of a team. A huge thank you to Curtis and Heather and all the Entangled Macmillan team who help make every story come to life. My gratitude is endless. Thank you to my marvelous agent Jill Marsal who is my guide and in my corner. And to all the friends who listen to me during the times when babbling on about books is absolutely necessary.

About the Author

USA Today bestselling author Eva Devon was raised on literary fiction, but quite accidentally and thankfully, she was introduced to romance one Christmas by Johanna Lindsey's Malory novella, *The Present*. A romance addict was born. She devoured every single Lindsey novel within a few months and moved on to contemporary and paranormal with gusto. Now, she loves to write her own roguish dukes, alpha males and the heroines who tame them. She loves to hear from her readers.

Discover more romance from Entangled...

Make Mine a Marquess
a Daring Ladies novel by Tina Gabrielle

Everyone thought that the Marquess of Landon was lost at sea. Instead, Robert Kirkian survived and has returned to London to reclaim his title from the man who tried to have him killed: his cousin. But proper vengeance requires patience—and the perfect weapon. Miss Phoebe Dawson is everything an ambitious gentleman could desire in a wife. Phoebe knows that love is a fool's game, even if the Marquess does play his hand like an expert. But she's about to discover the only thing more dangerous than a rogue is a wronged man hellbent on revenge...

How Not to Hate a Duke
a novel by Jennifer Haymore

Georgiana Milford may be a wealthy heiress without a title, but even *she* has her limits. During a party at a lord's country home, she's forced to endure her father's greatest enemy: *the Duke of Despots*. Nothing tempts the scoundrel in Theo St. Clair more than the prospect of kissing the prim-and-proper-ness right off Georgiana Milford's lovely lips... Now they're trapped together, forced to wear polite smiles while they trade acidic barbs and pretend to ignore the growing tension charging the air between them. But while there is danger in ruin, it's the devastating secret her family has been hiding that will shatter Georgiana's world...